"I like it better when Morrison."

"What else do you like?"

Bracing his hands against the door, fencing her in, Morrison gazed intently at her, his deep brown eyes smoldering with desire. Inwardly chastising herself for her salacious quip, Karma sucked in a breath. *Why did I say that? Why am I flirting with a man who is totally out of my league?* Her loose lips had gotten her into trouble, and the longer he stared at her the harder her limbs shook. Her head was spinning, but she projected confidence, not fear, and said, "Thank you for a wonderful evening, Morrison. Good night."

"It's midnight," he announced, lowering his mouth to her face. "Happy birthday, beautiful. I hope this year brings prosperity, excitement and adventure. They don't call it the dirty thirties for nothing, so throw caution to the wind and own every moment."

Shivering as his lips moved gently against hers, she willed her legs not to buckle. Deep down, she craved his touch, his kiss, but she wasn't brave enough to make the first move.

"Life is not remembered in days, Karma. It is remembered in moments, and this moment will remain with me forever."

Dear Reader,

Karma Sullivan and Morrison Drake are opposites in every sense of the word. The only thing they have in common is their mutual dislike! That's what makes *Pleasure in His Kiss* such a delicious read. After a passionate first kiss, Morrison can't get the sultry salon owner out of his mind. The no-nonsense judge sets his sights on Karma, and she isn't strong enough to resist his seductive charms. I hope you have fun "watching" Karma and Morrison flirt at a ritzy New York City wedding, enjoy their romantic marathon date at beautiful Coopers Beach and root for them despite the obstacles in their way.

Kimani readers, I can't thank you enough for your support and encouragement over the years. I'd love to hear what you think of Karma and Morrison's sizzling love story, so connect with me at pamelayaye@aol.com, or on my social media pages.

All the best in life and love,

Pamela Yaye

Pleasure in His Kiss

Pamela Yaye

HARLEQUIN® KIMANI™ ROMANCE

Recycling programs
for this product may
not exist in your area.

ISBN-13: 978-1-335-21671-7

Pleasure in His Kiss

Printed in U.S.A.

Pamela Yaye has a bachelor's degree in Christian education. Her love for African American fiction prompted her to pursue a career in writing romance. When she's not working on her latest novel, this busy wife, mother and teacher is watching basketball, cooking or planning her next vacation. Pamela lives in Alberta, Canada, with her gorgeous husband and adorable, but mischievous, son and daughter.

Books by Pamela Yaye

Harlequin Kimani Romance

Evidence of Desire
Passion by the Book
Designed by Desire
Seduced by the Playboy
Seduced by the CEO
Seduced by the Heir
Seduced by Mr. Right
Heat of Passion
Seduced by the Hero
Seduced by the Mogul
Mocha Pleasures
Seduced by the Bachelor
Secret Miami Nights
Seduced by the Tycoon at Christmas
Pleasure in His Kiss

Visit the Author Profile page
at Harlequin.com for more titles.

Chapter 1

Karma Sullivan didn't know who was shouting inside her swank, full-service beauty salon, Beauty by Karma, but she was going to find out. Balancing the books would have to wait. Her customers were probably having a spirited discussion about sex and relationships, but things had obviously gotten out of hand. It sounded as if World War Three had broken out on the main floor, and since nothing mattered more to Karma than maintaining the elegance and dignity of her salon, she dropped her pen on the April spreadsheets, and shot to her feet.

Her gaze fell on the mahogany desk across the room, and her shoulders sagged. Karma could only wonder where Jazz was. She'd met Jazmine "Jazz" Figueroa at cosmetology school six years earlier, and they'd bonded over their love of fashion, pop culture, Idris Elba movies and exotic cuisine. Hiring the gregarious esthetician to be the manager of her beauty salon was a no-brainer. Karma enjoyed working alongside her bestie, and thought they made a formidable team. Unfortunately, her happiness had been short-lived. Jazz used to be a model employee, who gave a hundred percent to Beauty by Karma, but these days she came to work late, spent more time on her cell than with clients and left early. And when Karma spoke to Jazz yesterday about her concerns she'd mumbled an apology, then quickly changed the subject.

A deep, husky voice filled the air, yanking Karma out of her thoughts and back to the present. What in the world? Has everyone lost their minds? Beauty by Karma was a ritzy, high-end salon in the Hamptons, not a barbershop in the hood, and she wasn't going to let anyone ruin the peaceful ambience. Since the salon's grand opening, Karma had worked tirelessly to get her business off the ground, and her efforts had paid off. She had A-list clients, a successful beauty blog millennials couldn't get enough of and tens of thousands of social media followers.

Yanking open her office door, she marched down the hallway, her lush, purple-hued tresses cascading around her shoulders. She'd paired her short, off-the-shoulder sundress with gold accessories, and even though she'd gained weight while vacationing with her girlfriends in the Cayman Islands in January she felt beautiful in the flowy, Gucci dress. Still, she was starting The Raw Food after her birthday. Yesterday, she'd received an email from the Hamptons Women's Association informing her she'd been nominated for the Businesswoman of the Year award, and Karma had been so excited she'd danced around her office. Wanting to look fit and fabulous for the July banquet, she'd hired a personal trainer, and was going to eat healthy for the next three months even if it killed her. And it would. Karma loved junk food, drank wine every night with dinner and was a self-proclaimed chocoholic. The last time she'd exercised Obama was still in office, and when her trainer suggested Karma take an aerobics class five days a week she'd burst out laughing. It was going to be hard going to the gym and changing her poor eating habits, but Karma was determined to get in shape.

Classical music was playing in the background, but it did nothing to soothe her mind. Karma loved hip-hop music, could rap with the skill and finesse of Yeezy, but since her customers preferred Bach to Kanye West, that was what they listened to during business hours.

Entering the salon, a smile curled her lips. The grand opening was eighteen months ago, but every time she entered the shop she felt a rush of pride. Beauty by Karma was her "baby," the only thing that mattered to her. Decorated with comfort and luxury in mind, the space had chandeliers dripping with crystals, cushy designer chairs and exquisite African artwork. Glass vases filled with colored roses beautified the twenty-five-chair salon, and black-and-white photographs of her celebrity clients were hanging on the mauve walls.

There was a buzz in the air, and when Karma saw the chocolate hottie standing at the reception desk, she understood why every woman in the salon—including the cosmetic heiress, a trophy wife and a marketing executive—were licking their lips and fanning their faces.

Someone whistled, and Karma overheard a Broadway actress murmur in Spanish, *"¡Señor, si tuviera un hombre que se pareciera a eso en casa, nunca dejaría la casa!"* A giggle tickled her throat. *I agree*, she thought, hiding a smirk behind the stoic expression on her face. *You're right! If he was my man I wouldn't leave the house, either!*

Her legs wobbled, as if they were about to give way, but she didn't lose her footing on the gleaming, hardwood floor. Caught off guard by her physical attraction to the man with the chiseled face and muscled body, she couldn't think or speak. Was at a loss for words. Shocking, considering Jazz had affectionately nicknamed her Yabbermouth the day they met, but when he glanced in her direction Karma's tongue fell limp in her mouth. Having worked on magazine photo shoots and music videos, she was used to meeting attractive men, but the longer she stared at him the harder it was to control her X-rated thoughts. Suddenly, perspiration drenched her forehead and breathing was a challenge.

Karma checked him out on the sly. The man had it all. Flawless, cocoa-brown complexion? *Yes.* Perfect teeth and a defined jawline? *Yes.* Boyish good looks, and more muscles than Dwayne "The Rock" Johnson? *Yes, yes, yes!* There weren't enough words in the English language to describe how gorgeous he was, and for a moment Karma was starstruck, consumed with desire. He was wearing a striped polo shirt, knee-length shorts and white sneakers, but he carried himself like a man in a designer suit, and Karma was so anxious to meet him she moved through the salon faster than an Olympian speed walker.

"You have to do something," the stranger fumed, addressing the receptionist. "This is important. *Very* important. I wouldn't be here if it wasn't."

His cologne, like his voice, was captivating, and listening to him made Karma tingle from her ears to her toes. Swallowing hard, she mentally chastised herself. Told herself to get a grip, and quit lusting after the man with the piercing gaze and ripped physique.

Joining the receptionist, Abigail Reese, behind the front desk, Karma offered her right hand in greeting, even though she knew touching him would push her horny body over the edge. Driven to succeed, she'd put her career above her personal life, and although her girlfriends teased her about being celibate, Karma loved being single and had zero desire to settle down. Why would she? Relationships sucked, and her ex-boyfriend had proved that even humble, sensitive men with good reputations couldn't be trusted.

Her gaze returned to the stranger's face, and zeroed in on his thick lips. *Oh my. I bet they could do some serious damage.* Tingles flooded her body, pricking her skin. Karma couldn't remember the last time she'd had sex, but if Mr. Tall-Buff-and-Dreamy invited her to his place she'd say yes in a heartbeat. It was an outrageous thought, considering she didn't even know his first name, but her body had a mind of its own, and it wanted his hands in her hair, on her breasts and between her legs—

"Who are you?"

Startled by his curt tone, Karma broke free of her thoughts and met his gaze.

"Hello," she said brightly, ignoring the butterflies in her stomach. "I'm Karma Sullivan, the owner of this fine establishment. How may I help you?"

"You're the owner? Finally. It's about time you showed up."

Ice spread through Karma's veins, chilling her to the bone. Put off by his cold demeanor, she dropped her hands to her sides, and pinned her shoulders back, radiated confidence even though his rigid stance was intimidating. "What can I do for you, sir?"

"I'm Morrison Drake, Reagan's uncle..."

He reached into his back pocket, took out his wallet, then raised his driver's license in the air. Scanning it, Karma committed the details to memory. According to the information on the card, he was six feet six inches, two hundred and twenty-five pounds, with dark brown hair and eyes. Morrison was thirty-four years old, and he was born on...August 2...

Overcome with emotion, sadness stabbed her heart.

Morrison shares the same birthday as my mom. Needing a moment to gather herself, she took a deep, calming breath. Thinking about Carmelita's tragic death six years earlier always made her cry and since she didn't want to break down at the salon, she willed herself to keep it together.

A troubling thought ran through her mind. Was Reagan okay? Was she in trouble? Needing more help at, Beauty by Karma, she'd hired the high school senior as a salon associate weeks earlier, and already had a soft spot for the teen. Karma straightened her bent shoulders and tried her best to recall everything Reagan had ever said about her uncle, Judge Morrison Drake.

Uncle Morrison is serious, stubborn and strict, she'd complained, one evening last week when they were cleaning the salon after closing. *He rarely laughs or smiles, but I hope he finds a girlfriend soon, because I'm sick of him running my life. I'll be eighteen in July, Ms. Karma. I should be able to do what I want, and go as I please...*

Bits and pieces of other conversations they had filled her mind and, as Morrison glared at her, Karma suspected everything Reagan had told her about him was true. She had her work cut out for her, knew it was going to be hard to turn his scowl into a smile, but Karma was up for the challenge. "It's a pleasure to meet you, Mr. Drake. Welcome to Beauty by Karma."

He nodded, but didn't speak. Stared at her as if he was bored out of his mind.

"Reagan tricked me," Karma said, hoping to lighten the mood with a joke. "You're tall, dark and handsome. There's no way you're a tyrant!"

Morrison didn't laugh. Instead, his frown deepened, and his lips formed a hard line.

"Is Reagan here? Have you seen her? Do you know

where she is?" he asked, his gaze darting around the salon. "Your employees won't tell me anything and it's infuriating."

Karma shook her head. "No, she's not here. Why? What's going on?"

"Reagan didn't come home last night, and I'm worried about her."

"Are you sure? Maybe she got home late, and left before you woke up."

"I checked the alarm history. I set it before bed, and it was never deactivated."

"Have you tried calling her?"

"Of course, I've tried calling her," he snapped, his frustration evident by his sharp tone. "But every time I call, her cell goes straight to voice mail. Worse, she hasn't responded to any of my text messages, and none of her friends know where she is, either."

His voice cracked, faltered under the weight of his emotions, and his demeanor softened. As Karma watched Morrison pace the length of the waiting area, his head bent, his hands balled into fists, two things became abundantly clear: he was angry, and he was scared. Filled with sympathy, Karma wanted to help. All of her employees knew and loved Reagan, and she did too. Treated her like the kid sister she'd always wanted, but didn't have—

"How long has my niece been working here?"

Caught off guard by the question, seconds passed before Karma spoke. "A month."

"A month?" he repeated, stopping abruptly. "Are you kidding me?"

His gaze was full of confusion, but Karma didn't know why. Couldn't understand why he was shouting at her. Wondered why he was staring at her in disgust.

Morrison gestured to the reception desk with a flick

of his head. "My niece came in here, filled out an application, and you didn't think it was important to contact me before offering her a job?"

"No, Reagan's almost eighteen, and her CV was impressive—"

Before she could finish her thought, Morrison cut her off midsentence.

"You should have called me. If I didn't go into Reagan's room this morning, and snoop through her things, I wouldn't even know she worked here. Thank God I found a pay stub in her desk, or I'd still be in the dark about her having a part-time job."

Karma winced, couldn't believe Morrison had invaded his niece's privacy, and had the nerve to look proud of himself, as if he'd made a three-point basket from half-court with his eyes closed. Feeling the need to defend herself, she said, "I rarely hire high school students to work in my salon, because they're often unreliable, but I'm glad I took a chance on Reagan. She's a wonderful young lady, and a model employee."

Morrison snorted, then argued that a beauty salon was no place for a teenager.

Karma pursed her lips together and swallowed the fiery retort on the tip of her tongue. She treated everyone who entered her salon—from the delivery person to the relentless salesperson—with respect, and whenever her staff complained about clients, Karma would quote her mother's favorite saying. *Kindness is never wasted*, she'd quip in a singsong voice, but Morrison was working her last nerve and Karma wanted him gone. Wished she could grab him by the ear and heave him out of her salon. Karma liked four-letter words and used them often, especially when she was driving on the freeway, but everyone in the salon was listening in on their conversation and if she cursed Morrison out her staff would never let her live it down.

"I couldn't have asked for a better employee and I'm thrilled Reagan's part of the Beauty by Karma family," she continued, speaking from the heart. "She's a smart young woman with a great head on her shoulders and a very bright future in the cosmetology field."

"Cosmetology?" Morrison scrunched up his nose as if someone had tossed a stink bomb through the window. "Reagan's going to university in the fall, not beauty school."

Karma raised an eyebrow, but wisely said nothing, knowing it would only make things worse if she told Morrison that his niece had changed her mind about becoming a lawyer and wanted to become a makeup artist instead. Karma should know. She'd helped Reagan fill out applications for cosmetology school weeks earlier, and written recommendation letters for her, as well. Unique and creative, with boundless enthusiasm, Reagan had raw, natural talent, and with the right training could one day be a household name in the makeup industry.

The telephone rang, and Karma picked it up, feigning excitement even though she was annoyed with Morrison-I-Think-I-Am-The-Boss-Drake. Thankful for the interruption, she chatted for several minutes with the celebrity publicist and penciled her name in the leather-bound appointment book for tomorrow morning. Her schedule was jam-packed, filled with so many bookings she'd have to work through lunch, but Karma wouldn't have it any other way. For years she'd dreamed of owning a beauty salon and, thanks to the kindness of her A-list clients, Karma was the go-to hairstylist and makeup artist in the Hamptons. *I wish my mom was alive to see me today. She'd be so proud of everything I've accomplished—*

"Is Reagan working today?"

Karma consulted the appointment book, saw Reagan's name at the bottom of the weekly schedule, and nodded. "Yes, but not until ten o'clock."

"Good, I'll wait," he announced. "And, if she doesn't show up I'm calling the police."

Panic streaked across Abigail's heart-shaped face, and Karma knew they shared the exact same thought: *Hell no! He can't stay here for an hour!* Karma opened her mouth to suggest Morrison go grab a coffee at the café across the street, but she thought better of it. Didn't want him to think he wasn't welcome at the salon. He wasn't, especially when he was insulting her and shouting at her staff, but since she didn't want to make any enemies in the small, tight-knit community, she racked her brain for another solution to her problem.

Her gaze strayed to the red, high-heel-themed clock hanging above the front door. Karma didn't have time to babysit Reagan's uncle. She had to finish balancing the books, update her website and blog, and when Jazz showed up she wanted them to talk. Had to find out what was going on with her best friend. Karma had work to do, and lots of it, but she feared what would happen if she left Morrison in the waiting area. What if he picked a fight with someone? Or insulted her staff? Or worse, caused a scene when Reagan arrived for her shift? Left with few options, she said, "Mr. Drake, let's speak in private. I can tell you more Reagan's job description, and give you a copy of her monthly schedule, as well."

Abigail sighed in relief, and Karma winked at her, wanting the single mom to know she understood her frustrations. It was hard to find good staff, and she wanted her employees to know she supported them wholeheartedly.

"Relax, relate, release," Abigail chanted in Karma's

ear, gently rubbing her back. "If you need me, text me 9-1-1, and I'll come running."

Karma swallowed a laugh. Her employees were the heart and soul of her business. They were her family, the brothers and sisters she'd never had, and Karma could always count on them to have her back, especially when she was dealing with hotheads like Morrison Drake.

"I don't want my niece working here, so consider this her two-week notice."

"With all due respect, Mr. Drake, that's not your decision to make."

"I'm Reagan's legal guardian, and what I say goes."

His tone was so cold, Karma shivered, but she didn't shrink under his withering glare.

"Maybe at the courthouse, but not here. This is my business, Mr. Drake, and I don't appreciate you causing a scene," she said in a quiet voice, even though she was fuming.

Surprise covered his face, and his eyebrows shot up his forehead.

That's right, she thought, feeling triumphant. *This is my spot, and I call the shots around here, Mr. Bossy Pants, not you.* Resisting the urge to dance around the desk, she forced a smile. "We can discuss the matter further in my office while we wait for Reagan to arrive, or you can leave. It's your choice."

"There's nothing to discuss. Reagan should be doing her homework, not doing nails, washing hair and sweeping floors. She's a Drake. It's beneath her…"

The murderous thought that popped into Karma's mind must have darkened her face because Morrison broke off speaking. "Oprah was a grocery store clerk before she became famous, Brad Pitt wore a chicken costume and Barack Obama's first job was at Baskin-

Robbins. You should be teaching Reagan to be humble, not proud and pompous."

"You misunderstood what I said—"

"No, I didn't," she snapped, cutting him off. "I heard you loud and clear."

Music filled the air, a strong, infectious beat that drowned out the noises in the salon.

"I have to take this call," he said. "It's my brother. Hopefully he's heard from Reagan."

Recognizing the chart-topping song, Karma couldn't resist swaying her hips to the music, and tapping her feet.

Fishing his iPhone out of his back pocket, Morrison touched the screen with his index finger, then put his cell to his ear.

Morrison liked Jay-Z? He listened to rap music? No way! He had a stern, no-nonsense demeanor, but hearing his ring tone made Karma think she'd pegged him all wrong. Maybe he wasn't an uptight jerk, she thought, giving him the once-over again.

Intrigued, Karma studied him closely. Everything about him was sexy—the way he talked, the way he carried himself, his commanding presence—but he wasn't her type. Karma liked men with tattoos and dreadlocks, who had a wild, adventurous side. Still, there was something about Morrison that appealed to her, that made her mouth wet and her heart race. Morrison Drake was the yummiest judge she had ever met, and if he wasn't bossy and short-tempered she'd give him her number. And more.

Karma waited patiently for Morrison to finish his phone call, and when he did she gestured for him to follow her. He did, and as they headed through the salon, Karma noticed they had an audience. Women ogled him from behind fashion magazines, handheld gadgets and hooded dryers. Walking with Reagan's drop-dead gorgeous uncle at her side gave Karma a dizzying rush, one she'd never experienced before and couldn't make sense of.

"Hey, Judge!" called a divorcée seated at the nail station. "Looking good!"

"If I was ten years younger I'd make you my second husband!" joked a single mom.

"Whooee!" hollered a reality TV star, her eyes wild with desire. "I've been a *very* bad girl, Judge Drake. Hold me in contempt of court in your private chambers!"

Cheers and raucous laughter erupted inside the salon. Karma glanced at Morrison, expecting to see a broad, grin spread across his face, but it wasn't there. To her surprise, Morrison looked concerned, not pleased that he had the attention of everyone in the salon, and Karma knew he was thinking about his niece. Had to be. That's why he'd driven over to the salon and stormed inside. Because he was scared Reagan was in trouble.

Feeling guilty for asking him to leave, Karma decided to do everything in her power to help Morrison find Reagan—including contacting her ex-boyfriend, Sergeant J. T. Garver at the Southampton Town Police Department. He'd broken her heart, and Karma regretted dating the cop for nine months, but she'd swallow her pride and make the call.

Chapter 2

Morrison didn't like Karma Sullivan. Didn't trust her. Sensed she was lying to him about his niece's whereabouts, but since he didn't have any proof of her deception he quit interrogating her. But if Reagan didn't show up at the salon for her ten o'clock shift he was going straight to the police station. It didn't matter that she hadn't been missing for twenty-four hours. Screw policies and procedures. Having worked in the judicial system for over a decade, Morrison knew how important it was to trust his instincts, and something told him Reagan was in trouble.

Considering the last time he'd spoken to his niece, Morrison tried to recall every detail of their conversation. Yesterday, he'd worked late, and as he was leaving the courthouse Reagan had called to say she was going bowling with some of her classmates. Before he could get more details, she'd hung up. Regret filled him. Morrison wished he'd taken the time to find out who his niece was with. He'd had dinner with his colleagues, then went straight home to bed. That morning, after finding Reagan's empty room and checking the alarm, he'd reached out to her friends but no one had seen her. If not for his family, insisting that he was overreacting, he would have already called the police. Morrison hoped he didn't end up regretting his decision.

A worrying thought ran through his mind. Was Reagan hurt? Had she been in a serious car accident? Was she lying unconscious in a hospital bed? Was that why she hadn't come home last night? His younger brothers, Duane and Roderick, thought he was blowing things out of proportion, but Morrison couldn't shake the feeling that something was wrong. That morning, when he'd called his family in a panic, his father, the Honorable Nathaniel A. Drake, reminded him that Reagan was almost an adult, and encouraged him to loosen the reigns. To stop treating her like a child. Morrison disagreed with his dad, told him he was wrong. Reagan was living under his roof and he expected her to abide by the rules, or else.

"I apologize in advance for the mess," Karma said, glancing over her shoulder as she sashayed down the hall, her long, wavy hair swishing across her back. "I share the office with my salon manager, and she'd rather surf the web than clean her desk."

Morrison gulped. He tried not to stare at her backside, tried not to notice how firm and plump it was, but it was hard to be a gentleman when she was walking in such a seductive way. Karma looked perfect, as if she'd just returned from an *Essence* magazine photoshoot, and it took every ounce of self-control he had not to touch her. But since he didn't want to get slapped, he buried his hands in the pocket of his tan, Dockers shorts and admired the mosaic wall paintings instead of her curves. Karma had the face of an angel, the juiciest set of lips he'd ever seen, and the moment she'd entered the salon she'd seized his attention. If he wasn't worried about Reagan, he'd skip his eleven o'clock tennis game at the Hamptons Sports Club with Duane and spend the rest of the day getting to know the titillating hairstylist with the mouthwatering cleavage. Morrison loved the female body almost as much as he loved his Fantasy Football League and imagined himself closing his eyes and burying his face in her big, beautiful breasts. Just thinking about it made his mouth wet and his erection rise inside his boxer briefs.

"Please, Mr. Drake, have a seat."

"No, thanks. I'll stand." He was polite, because it was in his nature, but he was pissed that his niece had been lying to him for weeks. And he didn't appreciate the things Karma had said, either. Imagine, his niece throwing away a full scholarship to one of the best universities in the country to attend cosmetology school. As if! It was the most ludicrous thing Morrison had ever heard, but he chose not to dwell on Karma's words. Booted them from his mind. She was dead wrong, and there was nothing she could say to convince him otherwise.

"Can I interest you in something to drink?"

Her smile was so bright it could light up Madison Square Garden, but Morrison reminded himself that Karma was the enemy, not an ally, and shook his head. Thinking about what she'd done made his eyes narrow and his jaw clench. The irresponsible salon owner had hired his young, impressionable niece to work in her beauty shop—a place where women openly talked about sex, bashed and ridiculed men, and God knew what else—and if he had his way Reagan would never step foot in the salon again.

"Mr. Drake, sit down. You'll be fine," she said, gesturing to one of the printed armchairs in front of her oval, glass desk. "I don't bite."

Morrison didn't move. Stayed put beside the door, listening for the sound of Reagan's voice in the salon. Folding his arms across the chest, he surveyed the bright and spacious corner office. Morrison had never seen so much pink in his life. It was everywhere—on the area rugs, the graphic wall art, the floor lamps and chalkboard walls. One side of the room looked as if it had been hit by a cyclone, and the other side was so clean he could eat off the floor. The office smelled of peppermint tea and cinnamon, and his mouth watered at the tantalizing aroma in the air. In his haste to leave the house, he'd forgotten to have breakfast and now his stomach was growling so loudly he'd bet Karma could hear it. That's why she was wearing a sad smile. Because she felt sorry for him.

"Are you sure I can't get you something to eat or drink? The staff room fridge is packed with healthy, delicious foods, and I hate to brag but I make a *mean* vegetarian omelet."

"No, thank you. I'm fine." It was a lie—he was hungrier than an NFL linebacker at an all-you-can-eat buffet, but Morrison didn't want to inconvenience her. Furthermore, he was at the salon to find Reagan, not to break bread with the overtly sexy owner. To keep his mind off Reagan he needed a distraction, and Karma Sullivan was it. His mother, famed interior designer to the stars, Viola Drake, always said, *A wise man learns many things from his enemies*, and Morrison planned to. Something was going on with his niece, and Karma was going to tell him everything he needed to know. He'd noticed a change in Reagan weeks earlier, during their college road trip, and since returning home things had only gotten worse. Reagan had dyed the ends of her hair purple, swapped her baggy shirts and sweatpants for belly-baring tops and miniskirts, and broken curfew twice.

Realization dawned, striking Morrison harder than a

blow to the head. Now everything made sense. Why his niece was wearing fake eyelashes and jewelry to school; she was copying her boss, Karma Sullivan. And Morrison didn't like it one bit.

Noting the framed certificates, plaques and awards proudly displayed on the glass bookshelf, Morrison carefully admired each one. "Karma Felicity Sullivan," he said aloud, reading the name printed on the Business of the Year award. "I don't think I've ever met anyone named Karma. It's a very interesting name."

A smirk curled her lips. "So I'm your first? I'm honored."

Morrison choked on his tongue. Speechless, his mouth was dry and his thoughts were muddled. He was attracted to Karma, thought she was one of the most beautiful women he had ever seen, but he couldn't lose his focus. Had to get to the bottom of things, and to do that Morrison had to maintain his composure, not lose his cool.

"Despite living a block away from each other as kids, my parents didn't meet until they were adults, and got pregnant with me on their first date," she explained. "My mom loved astrology and thought Karma was the perfect name for me. I think so too. You'd be amazed at how many compliments I get."

I believe it. You're stunning. I bet men chase you down 24/7!

"Tell me more about yourself, Miss Sullivan. I grew up in this town, so I know everyone except you. What brought you to the Hamptons, and how long have you lived here?"

A pensive expression covered her face, but her voice was full of warmth and excitement. As she spoke about growing up in Brooklyn, her years in beauty school and her dead-end jobs after graduation, Morrison found himself impressed with her rags-to-riches story. She'd created a lucrative business through dedication, hard work and sheer willpower and he was impressed by her inner strength. Karma gushed about her family, credited her mother and grandmother for her success, and he was moved by her gratitude for her loved ones.

"I was hired to do hair and makeup for the reality TV show *Hamptons Housewives* a few years back and because of the ridiculous popularity of the show I was able to quickly build my clientele," she explained, sitting back comfortably in her leather executive chair. "I opened this salon eighteen months ago, and if everything goes according to plan I'll open locations in Washington, Philadelphia and Chicago within the year."

"That's an incredible story," he said. "Congratulations on your success."

A proud smile filled her red-painted lips. "Thank you. I feel fortunate to be doing what I love. Not everyone is so lucky."

"I agree. I meet people every day who hate their jobs, and I can't help but feel sorry for them. I love what I do, and I couldn't imagine ever doing anything else."

"Me too! I love doing hair and makeup so much I'd work for free!"

Like the blast from a trumpet, her laugh was loud and lively. Cultured, and well-read, Karma was a great conversationalist with a zest for life. Morrison enjoyed learning about her educational background, her beloved shop and her favorite clients. Proud of her Jamaican–Puerto Rican heritage, Karma spoke fondly of her small, close-knit family from Brooklyn.

"Is it possible Reagan's with her dad, or another relative and forgot to tell you?"

"No, it's impossible. Reagan doesn't know who her

biological father is." Morrison didn't know if Karma was genuinely trying to help or fishing for information, but he suspected it was the latter. Still, he spoke his mind. "Reagan has loving grandparents, aunts and three doting uncles who adore her, but if she ever wanted to track down her biological father we have the money and resources to make it happen."

Peering out the door, Morrison glanced up and down the hallway for any sign of his niece, but he didn't see the teen anywhere. His fear intensified with each passing second, and if Karma hadn't persuaded him to come to her office he'd still be pacing in the reception area, worrying himself to death. "Do you see your parents often?" he asked, admiring the photographs hanging above the couch. "Do they still live in Brooklyn, or have they relocated here, as well?"

The light in her eyes faded. "No, they passed away in a car accident six years ago."

"I'm sorry for your loss," he said, filled with sympathy.

"Me too. My mom was my hero, and I definitely wouldn't be the woman I am today without her."

"Unfortunately, I know how you feel. I lost my…"

Painful memories of his sister, Emmanuelle, overwhelmed his mind and he lost his voice. His temperature climbed, and his limbs shook. Worried he'd succumb to grief and his knees would buckle, he dropped down in the padded armchair in front of Karma's desk. He wanted to tell her about his sister's death, but feared if he did he'd lose his composure. Morrison didn't feel comfortable baring his soul to her, so he said nothing. Pretended not to notice the sympathetic expression on her face. Damn, was his pain that obvious?

A chilling thought stole his breath. Had history repeated itself? Was his niece in grave danger? His heart stopped, and his pulse wailed in his ears like a siren. Had Reagan met the same fate as her mother? Was she... Morrison couldn't bring himself to say the word. Was scared that if he did his worst fear would be realized.

Standing, he straightened his bent shoulders. Coming to the salon had been a mistake. An error of judgment. He should have gone to the police station instead of wasting precious time at the beauty shop. Feeling guilty for sitting around with Karma, he hung his head. He'd never forgive himself if something bad happened to Reagan and hoped it wasn't too late to save her. He'd legally adopted her ten years ago and she meant the world to him.

"This was a mistake. I shouldn't be here. I should be at the police station."

Karma picked up her cell phone and glanced at the screen. "I can't believe it's already ten o'clock. I totally lost track of time," she said. "Morrison, wait. Let me check the salon one more time. If Reagan isn't here I'll call Sergeant Garver at the Southampton police station and get his advice."

"I know him. We play in the same recreational rugby league—"

Karma raised an eyebrow. "*You* play rugby?"

"And lacrosse, football and golf. What can I say? I'm a sports fanatic."

"Not me. I hate sports, and I can't imagine anything more boring than golf."

Clutching her cell phone with one hand, she tapped the screen with the other.

"How do you know Sergeant Garver?"

Shifting in her seat, Karma raked a hand through her hair, then flipped it over her shoulders. Morrison frowned. She was nervous. Why? What was she hiding?

"It's the Hamptons. Everyone knows everyone."

"That's not true," he countered. "Before today I had no idea who you were."

Karma shrugged. "That's because you're a bookworm who never goes out."

"I go out all the time. I enjoy eating out, hip hop concerts and sporting events—"

Hearing voices behind him, Morrison broke off speaking and glanced over his shoulder. Reagan! Relief flooded his body. Overcome with emotion, he pulled her into his arms for a hug. For the first time that morning, Morrison smiled. But when he remembered what his niece had done, how she'd scared him half to death, he released her. One minute. That's how much time Reagan had to explain herself, and if she lied to him she'd lose her privileges for three months. "Where have you been? I've been worried sick about you."

"I was at Zainab's house."

"Zainab? Who?" he asked, raising an eyebrow. "You've never mentioned her before."

"Zainab Qureshi. We met a few weeks ago at the mall, and hit it off."

Morrison slowly nodded his head, could feel the tension in his body recede as he listened to his niece. "I know her parents. Her father, Ibrahim, is an investment baron, and her mother is a jewelry designer. Her late grandfather was not only a former prime minister of Lebanon, but also one of the most influential businessmen in the world."

"Really? I knew her family was stupid rich, but I had no idea they were famous too."

"Where did you girls go last night, and why didn't you come home?"

"We fell asleep watching *Scream Queens*, and when

I woke up this morning my cell was dead and I didn't have my charger with me."

"Then why didn't you use Zainab's cell to call me? Was it dead too?"

"Unfortunately it was."

"How convenient," Morrison drawled, wearing a skeptical expression on his face. "They don't have a landline at their house?"

"House? They don't have a house. They have a gigantic, twelve-bedroom mansion dripping in gold, and it's so fly and flashy I want to move in—"

"Reagan, stop cracking jokes and answer my question."

"Uncle Morrison, no one has a landline anymore. That's *so* '80s. We're probably the only family in the state who still has one!"

"This is not funny. This is serious," he scolded. "I thought you were in danger."

"I was going to call you when I got here. I swear."

"Were Zainab's parents' home last night?" he asked, unsure of what to make of Reagan's story. "Can they confirm that you were there?"

"No, they're at the Monaco Yacht Show and won't be back until tomorrow. That's why I was at Zainab's estate last night. To keep her company."

Scrutinizing his niece's appearance, he searched for anything amiss. Her short hair was styled in tight, curls, her floral romper was clean and ironed, and her open-toe sandals added height to her petite frame. "I want Zainab's cell number, and Mr. Qureshi's number, as well."

"Why? That's so unnecessary, and embarrassing."

"Because I need to know the truth, and if I find out you lied to me you'll lose your car, your cell and your allowance for the next three months."

A gasp filled the room. "*Ouch*, don't you think that's a little harsh?"

"See," Reagan said in a self-righteous voice, propping her hands on her hips. "Ms. Karma thinks you're being unreasonable too."

Morrison glared at Karma, and to his surprise she glared back at him. Stared at him as if he'd lost his mind. Made him feel guilty, even though he'd done nothing wrong. What was her problem? Why was she scowling? Morrison wanted to ask her to leave, so he could talk to Reagan in private, then remembered they were in Karma's office and dismissed the thought.

"Is your cell charged now?"

Reagan shook her head. "No, but I can use one of the chargers in the staff room and text you their cell numbers later."

"Later? No. I want the information now."

"I can't. I'm at work, and since Ms. Karma doesn't like staff using their cell phones on the salon floor I'll message you when I take my lunch break."

"I don't want you working here. You should be at home studying for your midterm exams."

Her face fell, and panic flashed in her light brown eyes. "I—I—I can't quit. Ms. Karma needs me. Weekends are insane around here, and the staff can use all the help they can get."

Karma came around her desk, and stood beside Reagan. "She's right. We need her."

"Fine, you can stay, but today's your last shift. A beauty shop is no place for a kid—"

"I'm not a kid," she argued. "I'm a mature, young woman who's capable of making her own decisions, and I'm not quitting the best job I've ever had."

"It's the only job you've ever had," Morrison pointed

out, surprised by his niece's tone. Conflicted, he took a moment to consider his options. He didn't want to make a scene by dragging Reagan out of the salon, so he decided to let her stay. "We'll discuss this later."

"There's nothing to discuss. I'm staying at the salon, and there's nothing you can say to change my mind. I'm learning a lot, the staff is incredible and Ms. Karma is a terrific mentor."

Karma gave Reagan a one-arm hug, but Morrison wasn't moved. More convinced than ever that the hair and makeup artist was a negative influence on his niece he made a mental note to speak to his family about Karma Sullivan. His mom would know what to do, she always did. Morrison stuck out his hand. "I don't want you disappearing again, so give me your car keys."

"But, I didn't do anything wrong!" she argued. "It was an honest mistake."

"It's not open for discussion, Reagan. Hand them over, or you'll lose your cell too."

Reagan unzipped her shoulder bag and rummaged around inside for several seconds. Wearing a long face, she pulled out her key chain and dropped it in his palm. "I finish at six."

"That's ridiculous!" Morrison said, addressing Karma. "Why would you give my niece such a long shift? She's just a kid. Did *you* work eight-hour shifts when you were a teenager?"

"Yeah, I did. In fact, I worked thirty hours a week, *and* maintained a 4.0 GPA."

Reagan stared at Karma with stars in her eyes, and Morrison groaned inwardly. Damn. The last thing he wanted was for his niece to put the salon owner on a pedestal, but because of his blunder Reagan was gazing at Karma in awe, as if she'd just finished a death-defying stunt.

"I know Reagan is busy with school so she only works sixteen hours a week—"

"Sixteen hours a week," Morrison repeated, folding his arms rigidly across his chest. "So, all the times you told me you were going to the library to study you were here, doing hair and nails? Why did you lie to me? Why didn't you tell me you'd gotten a part-time job?"

"Because I knew you'd get mad. You always get mad when I don't do what you want, but I love working here and Ms. Karma says I'm talented."

Karma picked up a piece of paper from off her desk. "Here's a copy of Reagan's schedule for April, and May," she explained, speaking in a soft, soothing voice. "Look it over, Mr. Drake. If you're not happy with her shifts we can discuss it further."

"But I want to work more, Ms. Karma, not less."

Morrison scoffed. *If I have my way you won't be working here at all.*

"Here you go." Karma offered him the paper.

Morrison wanted to take the schedule and rip it to pieces, but he took the paper, folded it and stuffed it in his shirt pocket. "Reagan, I'll be back to pick you up at six o'clock."

"You will?" she asked, the disappointment evident in her voice. "But I thought you were going out with your friends tonight."

"Don't worry. I'm going, and you're spending the night with your grandparents."

"Lucky me," she drawled. "Can't wait."

Morrison kissed Reagan on the cheek. "Be good."

"I will. Have fun at the sports club," she said with a

wave. "Take it easy on Uncle Duane. He's a sleep-deprived dad of four, so don't beat him too bad!"

Morrison chuckled, but as he exited the office and marched through the salon, he wasn't thinking about his tennis match with his brother or his game strategy. He was thinking about Karma Sullivan—the sexy salon owner with the sensuous mouth and drool-worthy curves.

Chapter 3

An hour after leaving Beauty by Karma, Morrison parked his silver BMW X6 at the north entrance of the Hamptons Sports Club and took off his seat belt. He grabbed his water bottle and iPhone from the center console, and exited the SUV. Starving, he'd stopped at his favorite downtown café on the way to the sports complex and ordered the All-American breakfast. He'd left the family-owned restaurant with a smile on his face, a pep in his step and a full stomach. Now Morrison was ready for his tennis match, and confident he'd win.

A grin claimed his mouth. Duane was no competition; his brother would rather play video games in his free time, than sports, and Morrison suspected the only reason he'd agreed to meet up with him was to get out of the house. A brilliant software developer, with a hearty laugh and jovial personality, he'd quit his corporate job in the city so he could start his own business and spend more time with his family. Although he worked from home, Duane often joked about being a "househusband," but it was obvious he adored his sons and his pediatrician wife, Erikah.

Morrison retrieved his Nike duffel bag from the trunk, tossed it over his shoulder and activated the car alarm. The morning sun was overcast, filled with dark, fluffy clouds, and the air held the scent of rain. Approaching the outdoor tennis courts, Morrison heard balls bounce, cheers and groans, and the distant sound of pop music. The sports complex had it all, manicured grounds, knowledgeable staff and instructors, and an outdoor snack shop that served coffee, sandwiches and fruit.

Taking a deep breath quieted Morrison's mind, helping him to relax. He enjoyed the great outdoors, liked seeing the birds, the towering trees and the peaceful, picturesque views. Hearing his cell phone buzz, he fished it out of his pocket and read his newest text message. It was from his mom. Morrison felt guilty for not updating his family about Reagan. He should have phoned his mom from the car, instead of daydreaming about Karma Sullivan, but for some reason he couldn't get the salon owner out of his mind.

Morrison relived their conversation, dissecting everything Karma had said and done that morning. He was a great judge of character, could size up anyone in ten seconds flat, and he suspected Karma was a party girl who lived life by her own rules. The salon owner was a magnet, the kind of woman who attracted male attention wherever she went, the complete opposite of the females he usually dated. Still, he was intrigued by her, drawn to her. In her office, it took everything in Morrison not to touch her, and every time she looked at him he felt the urge to kiss her hard on the mouth. An hour after leaving the salon his body was still throbbing with need, but it was nothing a cold shower and a shot of Bourbon couldn't cure.

Typing fast, Morrison comprised a group text message

to his family, letting them know he'd found Reagan, and hit Send. The complex was crawling with sports enthusiasts but he didn't see his brother anywhere, and wondered if Duane had changed his mind about the game. Morrison played tennis three times a week, regardless of the weather, and was proud of his undefeated record. A fierce competitor with a passion for the game, he'd do anything to win, and he wasn't going to show his brother any mercy.

Strolling toward the tennis courts, Morrison saw children running around in circles, and a group of British nannies chatting in front of the water fountain. The women smiled and waved, and Morrison nodded in greeting. Glancing at his Gucci sports watch, he realized he was ten minutes late to meet his brother, and broke into a jog.

"Morrison Drake in the flesh? This must be my lucky day!" shrieked a female voice.

A brunette, in a red, lace-trimmed mesh dress, that looked more like lingerie than tennis attire, appeared in front of him, doing the happy dance. Morrison tried to move away but the woman was too fast. Pressing her body against his, she kissed him on each cheek. Her sickly sweet perfume made his eyes sting and his stomach churn.

Morrison thought hard. What was the woman's name again? She was one of his brother's fiancée's friends, and he vaguely remembered meeting her at Roderick and Toya's engagement party last summer. After a whirlwind courtship, his brother had popped the question to the twenty-five-year-old blonde from New Hampshire, and the couple were sparing no expense for their dream wedding. Roderick was an entertainment attorney who spent money like a Saudi prince, and the last time Morrison saw his youngest brother he'd bragged about booking Adele and John Legend to perform at the September ceremony.

"It's so great to see you again, Morrison," she gushed, her hand grazing his ass. "You look as handsome as ever. How have you been?"

Put off by how loud and aggressive she was, Morrison stepped back. He wanted to run for cover but remembered he was a Drake, not a pubescent boy, and gave a polite nod. Morrison couldn't believe how bold she was, and searched the grounds for the nearest escape route. "Great, thanks, and you?"

"Better, now that we're together," she purred, coiling a lock of frizzy hair around her index finger. "Join me inside for a drink. I just finished my private lesson, and my Swedish instructor worked me hard this morning. I could use something cold right now."

Morrison wore an apologetic smile, but deep down he was glad he had plans with his brother. Being one of the most eligible bachelors in the city certainly had its perks—single women dropped off home-cooked meals at his estate on a weekly basis, and he was invited to the best parties—but he was tired of pushy females propositioning him every time he left his mansion. "I'm sorry, I can't. I have a game, and if I leave my brother hanging he'll be pissed."

"I understand. Family comes first." Batting her extra-long eyelashes, she rested a hand on his forearm and squeezed it. "I bet you're an amazing tennis player, Morrison, so give me your number and we'll play one day next week. I'd love that, and I bet you would too."

Wrong again! He recalled how she'd bragged at Roderick and Toya's engagement party about dating a married New York senator. The brunette was the kind of woman who only cared about a man's status, and what he could do for her, and Morrison wasn't interested in seeing her again. Turned off by her overconfidence, and her skimpy attire, he said, "I have to go. I don't want to keep my brother waiting."

"Not so fast, mister. *You* have something I want." Sliding in front of him, she offered her cell phone, her eyes wide and bright. "Put your number in my cell, and I'll give you a ring later. Maybe we can hook up tonight."

He opened his mouth to decline her offer, but it was Duane's voice that filled the air.

"Are we gonna play or are you gonna stand around shooting the breeze?"

Morrison was so relieved to see Duane standing inside court nine he wanted to cheer. Moving with the quickness of an NFL running back, he dodged the brunette, entered the fenced court and closed the door behind him. He'd come to the sports complex to play tennis with his brother, not make a love connection. Besides, if he wanted to hook up with someone it would be a sophisticated and classy woman, like Karma. He wondered whom she spent her nights with, was curious if the salon owner had a man—

Morrison scoffed, telling himself he was being ridiculous. Of course, she was dating someone. Women like Karma, with brains, charisma *and* booty, didn't have one man, they had several, and he'd be a fool to pursue a woman who was playing the field. Not that he was ready to settle down. He wasn't. He had his hands full with Reagan, and aspirations of becoming the youngest Supreme Court judge in the nation. Not to mention aging parents who needed his help on a regular basis. His brothers were busy with their careers and families, and since he was the oldest— and happily single—he was the one who kept a watchful eye on their stubborn parents. His father was recovering from hip surgery, and these days his mother was so forgetful Morrison worried about her state of mind. They could afford to hire someone to help them, but they refused, saying they didn't want a stranger snooping around their waterfront estate.

"Did you get baby girl's number?" Duane teased, wiggling his thick eyebrows.

"Yeah, and I'm going to save it in your cell under Side Chick."

"Hey, don't joke about things like that!" Shivering, he pressed his eyes shut and made the sign of the cross on his chest. "Erikah has a quiet nature and a sweet disposition, but if she thought I was cheating on her she'd bury me alive."

"You better not, or I'll help her dig the ditch!"

Duane gave Morrison a shot in the arm, then dumped his Cleveland Cavaliers backpack at his feet. Short and stocky, with dark skin and a salt-and-pepper moustache, he was often mistaken for Morrison's older brother, and laughed off comparisons to their father.

"Ready to play?" Morrison unzipped his duffel bag and took out his tennis racket.

"Not yet. I need to stretch. Don't want to break anything."

Amused, Morrison watched his brother roll his neck from side to side, chuckling as Duane jogged in place for a minute, huffing and puffing as if he was climbing the Great Wall of China. Unlike Roderick, Duane would rather save money than spend it, but his workout gear had seen better days and Morrison couldn't resist teasing the dad of four about his faded Nike T-shirt and nylon basketball shorts. "After our game, I'm taking you to the mall. You need some new clothes ASAP, bro."

"Get out of here," Duane argued, wiping his forehead with the back of his hand. "This is the outfit I was wearing when I met LeBron James at Rucker Park several years ago, and since it always brings me good luck you don't stand a chance, Your Highness."

Morrison chuckled. "Not today, Daddy-Daycare! I'm going to mop the court with you."

Taking their positions on the court, they agreed to do practice shots to warm up, and took turns serving the ball. Morrison heard his cell phone ring from inside his duffel bag, but ignored it. He hadn't seen Duane all week, and he was having fun talking trash and joking around with his brother. His family meant the world to him, and nothing mattered more to Morrison than spending time with the people he loved. Losing Emmanuelle had been a crushing blow, the worst thing that had ever happened to him, and at her memorial service he'd vowed never to take his siblings for granted again.

"Reagan called me a few minutes ago, and she was really upset," Duane said. "You took her car keys? Why? She's an adult now, Mo, and it's time you start treating her like one."

"Duane, she's only seventeen. She still needs discipline and guidance and a strong, firm hand." Needing to vent, he told his brother about his trip to Beauty by Karma and his argument with Reagan. Morrison couldn't believe how much their niece had changed since he'd become her legal guardian. Five years ago, Reagan was a chubby seventh grader who loved Harry Potter and the Nickelodeon channel, and now she was obsessed with boys, makeup and social media. Worst of all, she was pulling away from him, and it hurt like hell.

"Mo, that's the second time this month you've gone off the deep end, and I'm worried if it happens again,

Reagan will leave for good, and none of us want to see that happen."

"Duane, relax. Reagan isn't going anywhere, and once she quits that stupid job at Beauty by Karma things will go back to normal."

"I don't know what your problem is. I love that place. Every time Erikah goes to get her hair and nails done, she comes home in a great mood." Duane winked. "And horny as hell!"

"That's the problem. A beauty salon is no place for a young, impressionable teenager like Reagan, and if Karma won't fire her I'll just have to take matters into my own hands."

"What are you going to do?"

Morrison wore a sly grin. "Use the Drake charm to get my way, of course."

"You sly dog!" Duane caught the ball midair with his right hand. "You asked Karma to be your date for Winston and Antoinette's wedding next Saturday, didn't you?"

He raised an eyebrow. Was Duane out of his mind? Had he been drinking? Morrison would rather catch up on sleep than attend the Manhattan wedding of his childhood friend, but it was going to be the social event of the year, and he couldn't skip it. Bringing a date was out of the question though. Born into wealth, the powerhouse couple had friends in high places, and political connections. And if Morrison wanted to achieve his goal of being the youngest person appointed to the Supreme Court he had to network his butt off, and everyone he wanted to meet would be at the wedding. "No way," he said, shaking his head. "Karma's not my type, and I don't want anyone to think we're a hot, new item—"

"Mo, get out of here, Karma's *everybody's* type. Who

doesn't want a smart, successful beauty on their arm? Shoot, if I wasn't happily married I'd be all over her."

"My focus is on Reagan right now, not hooking up with a feisty makeup artist."

"It should be. In the fall she'll be going off to college, and you'll be home alone with nothing to do and nowhere to go."

"Reagan's going to live at home, not on campus," he explained, nodding his head to emphasize his point. "Dormitories are dangerous, and I don't want her to get hurt."

"You worry too much. She'll be fine. Quit stifling her, or she'll rebel."

Morrison scoffed, not giving his brother's advice a second thought. "You know nothing about raising a teenager. Your kids are still in diapers, and they run you ragged!"

The brothers laughed.

"Go out with Karma," Duane advised, bouncing the ball absently on the court. "It'll be good for you. You need to quit hanging out at home 24/7 and get back in the dating game."

Ready to start their match, Morrison dropped to one knee and retied his shoelaces. "Are we going to play, or stand around talking about the ladies for the rest of the morning?"

"Neither. Let's go inside and grab a cold one. Erikah's forcing me to do a thirty-day cleanse with her, and I'm craving a beer. And French fries."

Morrison chuckled. "I'm glad I'm single. You're a sorry case, D!"

"And you're jealous," Duane countered, wearing a proud smile. "You wish you had a beautiful, sexy woman to come home to every night."

A vision of Karma dressed in a flimsy negligee and red-heeled pumps flashed in his mind. His thoughts took an erotic detour, filled with explicit images of the beauty salon owner with the silky, mile-long legs. Giving his head a shake, he tossed the tennis ball high in the air and smacked it powerfully with his racquet. "Game on."

"Mo, take it easy!" Duane shouted, running for cover as the ball whizzed past his face. "I'm a father of four, not a ten-time Wimbledon champion!"

Chapter 4

Morrison glanced at the clock on the dashboard of his SUV, realized he had an hour to kill before picking up Reagan from Beauty by Karma and contemplated visiting Roderick at his estate. He'd had so much fun at the sports complex with Duane, he was missing his youngest brother, and wanted to touch base with him. Two weeks earlier, during their monthly fishing trip to Shinnecock Inlet, they'd butted heads and their argument still left a bitter taste in Morrison's mouth. After downing one too many beers, Roderick had become loud and belligerent aboard Morrison's Scout 350, disrupting the serene and peaceful atmosphere. The gleaming, white vessel was the Mercedes-Benz of boats, and when Roderick threw up on the platform Morrison had lost his temper. Told Roderick he had a drinking problem and needed professional help. Filled with remorse, Roderick had agreed to pay for the boat to be detailed, but Morrison had yet to see a dime.

Hanging out with Duane had put him in a good mood, made him forget about his argument with Reagan at the beauty salon. For hours, he'd played in the hot sun, and by the time they went inside for lunch it was two o'clock.

What a match! Morrison thought with a wry smile. Duane had surprised him by winning the first game, but he'd battled back to win the next three. While eating burgers and fries, they'd talked about their parents, their careers and the groom's bachelor party next Friday. They were planning to drive to Manhattan together after work, and Morrison hoped Roderick could join them. These days, he didn't go anywhere without his bride-to-be, and Morrison was tired of Roderick putting his fiancée first and his family last. Toya Janssen had a girl-next-door vibe, but Morrison didn't think she was the right woman for his brother.

Arriving home that afternoon, Morrison had showered and changed into a short-sleeve denim shirt, blue jeans and navy loafers. After he dropped Reagan off at his parents' estate, he was meeting his poker buddies at The Long Island Bar & Grill and hoped they had some good news for him. Morrison needed his friends to work their connections and get him an invitation to the political fund-raising gala in Washington next month. It was the hottest ticket in town, and he had to be there. Couldn't afford to miss the exclusive, black-tie event. If he was lucky he'd meet the vice president, or his chief of staff. That's all Morrison needed. An introduction, and he'd be one step closer to making history.

Morrison narrowed his gaze. Gripping the steering wheel, he leaned forward in his seat. *What the hell?* Spotting Reagan exiting Beauty by Karma, he sped through the intersection. Pulling up to the curb, he lowered the passenger side window. "Reagan, where are you going?" he asked.

"Ms. Karma said I could leave early, and I didn't want to wait around for you."

Disappointment flooded his body. Morrison had hoped

to see Karma again. He'd convinced himself it was because he wanted to talk to her about his niece, but it was a lie. Sure, he wanted her to honor his request and fire Reagan, but he was attracted to Karma and wanted to get to know her better—especially in the bedroom. The salon owner was a vivacious beauty who wasn't afraid to speak her mind, and even though they'd butted heads that morning, he couldn't stop thinking about her. Fantasizing about her. Imaging them making love—

"You can leave. You don't need to wait around. Zainab's coming to pick me up."

"Why didn't you call me?"

"Because I'm not a baby. I can take care of myself."

"Get in. We can talk on the way to your grandparents' house."

Reagan tapped her foot on the ground, her arms crossed, her expression defiant. "No."

"Do you want me to confiscate your cell phone, as well?"

"I don't care," she answered, rolling her eyes skyward. "Do what you have to do."

His jaw clenched. She spoke in a clipped tone of voice, with plenty of attitude, infuriating him. Horns blared, but Morrison didn't move. He felt like an ass for holding up traffic, but he wasn't going anywhere until Reagan got into his SUV. He'd arranged to have her beloved car towed to his estate, and hoped his actions would send a powerful message to his niece.

Morrison put on his hazard lights, checked his rearview mirror for oncoming traffic and opened his door. Marching around the hood of the car, he struggled to control his temper. He was so intent on reaching Reagan, and talking some sense into her, he didn't notice Karma until she called his name.

"Morrison, what's going on? Is everything okay?"

Karma appeared on the sidewalk, wearing oval-shaped sunglasses and a bright smile.

One look at her was all it took. Instantly, his shoulders relaxed, and his anger receded. For the sake of peace, he said, "Reagan, please get in the car so I can drop you off at your grandparents' house. They're expecting you for dinner, and I don't want you to be late."

"Why do I have to go to their house? Why can't I stay home alone?"

"Because I'm going out with my friends, and I don't know when I'll be back."

"So?" she argued. "I can stay home alone. I'm seventeen, Uncle Morrison, not seven."

"I'd feel safer if you were with your grandparents."

"But I don't want to go. I want to stay home and relax."

"You can relax at Grandma and Grandpa's estate."

Reagan groaned. "This is so frustrating. Why do you keep treating me like a kid?"

"The last time I left you home alone you threw a raucous house party!"

"It wasn't a party. My friends came over, and we ordered pizza and listened to music."

"A hundred kids isn't a get-together, Reagan, it's a party."

Reagan mumbled under her breath.

"This isn't the time or the place to have this conversation," Morrison said, mindful of the people around them. The streets were busy, full of families and shoppers, and he didn't want anyone to overhear them. "Like I said, we can talk about this in the car, so get in."

Morrison opened the passenger side door and waited patiently for his niece to get in.

"I don't have to listen to you. I'm practically an adult. I can do what I want."

Stepping forward, Karma took Reagan by the shoulder and spoke to her in a quiet voice. "Sweetie, go with your uncle and work out your problems," she admonished, wearing a sympathetic expression on her face. "How can you fix what's wrong in your relationship if you don't talk to him?"

"Why bother? He doesn't listen to me," she complained.

"Real women don't run from their problems, they tackle them head-on." Karma helped Reagan into the SUV, then patted her hands. "I'll call you later to see how you're doing."

"Bye, Ms. Karma. Thanks again for lunch. It was delicious."

"My pleasure, sweetie. Next time I'll take you to the Peacock Alley at the Waldorf Astoria," she said, licking her lips. "Their brunch is to die for, and the waiters are supercute!"

Standing on the sidewalk, listening to his niece talk and giggle with Karma made Morrison smile. His admiration for the salon owner grew as he watched her interact with Reagan. Gregarious, and down-to-earth, it was easy to see why Reagan worshipped the ground Karma walked on. Her warmth and openness was endearing, what appealed to him most, and if they weren't polar opposites he'd take Duane's advice and ask her out.

Pressed for time, he marched back to the driver's door and got inside the SUV.

"Can I come by the salon on Wednesday?" Reagan asked, her eyes bright with excitement. "I'm Devin Skye's biggest fan ever, and I'd love to meet her."

"You're as sly as a ninja!" Karma teased. "I didn't tell

anyone about her appointment, so how did you know the actress was coming to the salon after closing?"

"I overheard you on the phone with her manager when I came to refill your coffee..."

Morrison opened his mouth to protest, to remind his niece that she had a physics test on Thursday she needed to study for, but thought better of it and held his tongue. He didn't want to upset her again, but made a mental note to talk to her about the test later. He loved Reagan as if she was his daughter and wanted to raise her the way his sister would.

Sadness pricked his heart. Emmanuelle had been gone for years, but Morrison missed her more each day. He tried not to think about her untimely death, only the good times, but as he listened to his niece joke around with Karma his emotions got the best of him and tears filled his eyes. Glad he was wearing sunglasses, he blinked them away. Not only was Reagan the spitting image of Emmanuelle, she had his sister's quick wit and her outrageous sense of humor.

"Please," Reagan pleaded, clasping her hands together. "I'll never ask you for anything again. I swear. It'll be my birthday present, and grad gift all rolled in one!"

"If it's okay with your uncle, it's okay with me."

Karma looked at Morrison, and their eyes locked, zoomed in on each other.

Pleased with her answer, he nodded his head in agreement. He spoke to Reagan, but his gaze was glued to Karma's face. "You can go to the salon as long as you finish your homework."

Reagan cheered. "Thanks, Uncle Morrison. You're the best!"

Karma beamed, and for some strange reason Morrison felt prouder than a gold medalist on a podium. Reagan spoke, but he missed her question because he was busy admiring Karma. Her curled eyelashes, bejeweled lavender nails and colored extensions didn't make her beautiful; it was her radiant smile and effervescent laugh that appealed to him. She waved, then turned and walked back into the salon, switching her shapely hips. Transfixed, he watched her every move. Wet his lips with his tongue. Groaned and grunted in appreciation.

"Uncle Morrison, snap out of it!"

Reagan waved a hand in front of his face, and Morrison blinked. Bolting upright in his seat, he put on his seat belt and started the car. Merging into traffic, he stepped on the gas and sped down the street. Anxious to get to his parents' house, he switched from one lane to the next, passing slow-moving vehicles and teens cruising the block in their flashy sports cars.

"So, you like Ms. Karma, huh?"

Morrison coughed to clear his throat. "Who, me?"

"Yeah, you. Want me to put in a good word for you?"

"Nice try, Reagan. I know what you're trying to do, but I'm not going to let you change the subject. What you did last night wasn't cool, and I'm very disappointed in you."

Hanging her head, she fiddled with her gold thumb ring on her left hand.

"Prove to me you can be trusted, and I'll give you more freedom."

"Sorry about last night, Uncle Morrison. It was an honest mistake. Really."

"I'm going to cut you some slack this time, but if you ever stay out all night you'll never drive your Mini Cooper again." Morrison opened the center console, took out Reagan's car keys and handed them to her. "Remember what I said."

"I will. Thanks, Uncle Morrison."

Driving along Main Street, he marveled at how much the Hamptons had changed since he was a kid. There were high-end restaurants, salons and boutiques popping up every week, and Morrison couldn't go anywhere without spotting the paparazzi lying in wait. Noticing a helicopter in the sky, which was the preferred mode of travel from New York for the very wealthy, he wondered who was flying in. In the summer, residents complained of the traffic, the noise and the party atmosphere, but Morrison was looking forward to socializing and networking with foreign businessmen and obscenely rich entrepreneurs.

"Can you please take me home? I'm tired, and I'd really like to chill out in my room," she explained. "I'll visit with Grandma and Grandpa tomorrow."

He took a moment to consider her request. "Fine, but I don't want anyone in the house. No friends, no loud music, and if you decide to go out you have to be home by curfew."

She sighed deeply, her eyes narrowed and her mouth twisted in a frown.

"I know you think I'm hard on you, but everything I do is for your good—"

"Okay, okay, I get it. From now on, I'll obey your every word. Now, back to you and Ms. Karma. When are you going to ask her out?"

Morrison kept his eyes on the road. "I don't know what you're talking about."

"Come on, Uncle Morrison, keep it a hundred." Facing him, she tucked her feet under her bottom and tapped an index finger against her cheek. "You're feeling her, and you know it. You were staring at her *hard* when she left. It's a miracle you didn't pop an eye vessel."

Morrison wanted to laugh, but he wore a straight face. He couldn't remember the last time he'd seen his niece this happy, and was amused by her jokes. The truth was out. He was interested in Karma, sexually attracted to her, but he'd never act on his feelings. His focus was on raising Reagan and advancing his career, not pursuing a feisty, provocative woman from Brooklyn.

Drumming his fingers on the steering wheel, he thought about his ex-girlfriend. Their relationship had ended because the anesthesiologist didn't get along with Reagan, and none of the females he'd met in recent months appealed to him. They were all savvy career women with graduate degrees, but there'd been no spark, no fire. Morrison realized he had the opposite problem with Karma. Their chemistry was so strong every time their eyes met he wanted to kiss her, to stroke every inch of her body. There was nothing sexier than a woman who was comfortable in her own skin, and Karma moved with the ease of a runway model.

"Uncle Morrison, you have to bring your A game to win Ms. Karma over and, even though you play chess and watch CNN religiously, I have complete faith in you."

Morrison scoffed, and Reagan giggled. He didn't mind her poking fun at him, and chuckled when she started clapping and singing off-key.

"Uncle Morrison and Ms. Karma sitting in a tree, *k-i-s-s-i-n-g*," Reagan sang, dancing around in her seat, her voice strong and loud. "First comes loves, then comes marriage, then comes triplets in a Gucci baby carriage!"

Wearing a wry smile, Morrison turned into his estate and drove up the driveway.

"Men are always hounding Ms. Karma for her number, so you have to come correct when you ask her out. And don't be late for your date. Ms. Karma hates that."

"Bye, Reagan," he said, unlocking the doors. "Don't forget to put on the alarm."

"I will. Bye, Uncle Morrison. See you later!"

Reagan threw open the door then rushed inside. Morrison was pressed for time, but he sat in his SUV for a moment, thinking about his conversation with his niece. She'd promised to be on her best behavior, but Morrison didn't believe her. To assuage his fears, he'd call Duane and ask him to check up on Reagan tonight.

Karma's words came back to him, playing in his ears like a song. *Mistakes are a part of growing up, and if you don't give Reagan the room to fall she'll never learn to fly.* He'd disagreed with Karma that morning in her office, still did. He knew what was best for Reagan, and his job was to protect her, to make sure she didn't make the same mistakes his sister did as a teenager. He'd convince Karma to fire Reagan, and when she did he'd show his appreciation—in the bedroom. Encouraged by the thought, Morrison drove back down the driveway, whistling to himself. Considering his next move, he broke into a broad grin as a plan formed in his mind. Karma was no match for him, and he'd prove it.

Chapter 5

"Girl, you're lucky I love you, or I'd steal your rich, fine-ass fiancé right from under your nose!"

The bridesmaids cackled at the matron of honor's outrageous joke, laughing as if they were watching a comedy special on the flat screen TV, and the bride rolled her eyes to the ceiling. The Royal Suite at the Four Seasons New York was so loud and noisy, Karma could feel a headache forming in her temples and took a deep breath to stop the room from spinning.

Scared her knees were going to buckle, Karma leaned against the padded armchair the bride was sitting on. For the past three hours, she'd been doing hair and makeup for the Tolbert-Lefevre bridal party—and discreetly blogging about it on her iPhone when no one was looking—and Karma was so tired all she could think about was taking a nap.

Her thoughts returned to that morning. The bride had called her in a panic at 6 a.m. because her long-time stylist had fallen ill and couldn't do her hair and makeup for her wedding. Torn over what to do, Karma had weighed the pros and cons of going to Manhattan. She'd wanted to help the White House deputy assistant, but she'd planned to spend her birthday weekend partying with Jazz in the city. But when the bride agreed to triple her fee, *and* pay for two nights' accommodations at the Four Seasons New York, Karma had accepted the job. Karma felt guilty for changing her plans with Jazz at the last minute, but she'd be a fool to turn down the high-paying gig. It had taken some convincing, but Jazz had agreed to meet her at the hotel after the reception, and Karma was looking forward to hanging out with her bestie tonight.

The gold wedding invitation card, propped up on the fireplace mantel, caught Karma's eye. Everyone who mattered in the world of business, politics, entertainment and sports would be at the Tolbert-Lefevre wedding, and Karma was hoping to find some new clients. The Hamptons' upper crust was starting to notice her, and it felt good. More than anything, she wanted Beauty by Karma to be a household name. That was the only way to honor her mother's legacy. Her mom's words played in her mind as Karma remembered happier times. *You're smart, and strong, and capable,* hermosa, *and you can do anything you put your mind to. You're destined for great things, so walk boldly into your destiny—*

"It's the moment we've all been waiting for," shrieked a pencil-thin bridesmaid, throwing open the suite door. "Breakfast is here, ladies, so eat now or forever hold your peace!"

Giggles and cheers filled the air as the bridal party swarmed the lanky waiter and his cart.

"I'm too nervous to eat," Antoinette confessed with a sheepish smile. "Last night at the rehearsal dinner, Winston fed me so much caviar and beignets I'm *still* full…"

Karma tucked her foundation brush in her vinyl makeup tool belt and picked up her water bottle. Taking a sip, her gaze wandered around the room. Bridesmaids were eating gooey pastries, snapping selfies and singing along to the R & B song playing on the Bose stereo system. The lavish suite occupied the top floor of the five-star hotel, and had all the amenities a guest would want. Eye-catching contemporary art, a champagne-filled mini-bar and a butler's kitchen worthy of a celebrity chef. Ornate chandeliers hung from twenty-six-foot ceilings, and the windows offered panoramic views of the city skyline.

Determined to finish strong, Karma took a deep breath and got back to work. Blocking out the noise in the suite, she cupped the bride's chin in her hand, and added waterproof mascara to her eyes. Karma had never dreamed of getting married, or being a wife, but she envied the forty-year-old bride from Long Island. Antoinette was living the American dream; she had a fantastic career, a supportive family and a doting fiancé. Karma had never been madly in love, or swept off her feet, and listening to Antoinette gush about her fiancé made Karma wish she had a soul mate too. Someone who would accept her in spite of her past.

For some strange reason, an image of Morrison flashed in her mind. At the thought of him, her mouth dried and her nipples hardened underneath her purple, silk shirtdress. Karma wondered how Judge Hottie was spending his weekend. Or rather, who he was spending it with. Since their run-in last Saturday at her shop she'd bumped into him twice. Once at the grocery store, and yesterday at the bank. She'd wanted to approach him, had even rehearsed what she'd say when they came face-to-face, but by the time Karma finished with the teller Morrison was gone. Not that it mattered. He thought he was better than her, so why waste her time flirting with him?

Karma added bronze blush to the bride's cheeks, concentrating intently on what she was doing so she wouldn't mess up, but Morrison consumed her thoughts. They were from two different worlds, and even though she was a successful businesswoman worth millions, she'd never be on his level. He had status and prestige, and she was a lowly stylist from Brooklyn; they didn't belong together, and Karma had a better chance of winning *Survivor* than hooking up with him. Still, she lusted after him. She'd thought she was doing a good job hiding her true feelings, but when Reagan stopped by the shop yesterday after school she'd said, *I'm glad you like my uncle, Ms. Karma. You're perfect for him.*

Karma shuddered at the memory. Mortified that her clients had overheard Reagan, she'd dragged the teen aside and set her straight, assured her that there was nothing going on between them. Though, deep down, Karma wished there was. She wasn't looking for love, and didn't want to get married or have children, but she was attracted to Morrison and couldn't stop thinking about him. Thanks to Reagan, she'd learned some interesting facts about Morrison. He spoke Spanish fluently, loved fishing and horror flicks, and most shocking of all, he was an avid traveler who had been to more than fifty countries.

"The photographer will be here in ten minutes," announced a baby-faced bridesmaid, checking out her reflection in the wall mirror. "Get yourselves together, ladies. It's showtime!"

A shriek went up in the suite, as bridesmaids rushed about, getting ready.

"You look incredible, Antoinette," Karma praised, adjusting the bride's diamond tiara. "Excited to become Mrs. Winston Tolbert?"

Antoinette touched her stomach, then cupped a hand over her mouth.

"Sweetie, what's wrong?"

"I think I'm going to be sick," she mumbled, her eyes wide with alarm.

Thinking fast, Karma helped the bride to her feet and into the bathroom.

"It's just your nerves acting up. You'll be fine."

"What if I'm not?" Antoinette paced the length of the room, her fuzzy, high-heel slippers slapping against the marble floor. "What if I'm making a mistake? What if things don't work out? What if Winston and I don't last?"

Over the years, Karma had done hair and makeup for hundreds of weddings, but this was the first time she'd ever seen a bride with cold feet—and it wasn't pretty. Antoinette had tears in her eyes, a runny nose and a panicked expression on her oval face. Jazz often joked that a stylist was a therapist, a mother and a pastor all rolled into one, and as she listened to Antoinette vent, Karma realized her bestie was right. She had to find a way to calm her down, fearing if she didn't the deputy assistant would be a runaway bride.

Filled with compassion, she wore a sympathetic smile. Though she'd only met the groom a couple times, Karma liked him and thought he was the perfect counterpart for Antoinette. And if anyone could have a successful marriage, it was the bold, adventurous couple.

The door flew open, and the matron of honor paraded inside, carrying two flutes overflowing with champagne. "Sis, it's not too late to change your mind," she trilled, shoving a glass into the bride's hands. "Just kidding! You have to marry Winston. He's the only man I know who'll put up with your crap!"

"Shut up, Bianca. No one asked you," Antoinette snapped. "Just go. I don't want you in here."

Her laughter stopped, and the smirk slid off her heart-shaped face. "Relax, sis, I was just teasing."

Wanting a moment alone with the bride, Karma gripped the matron of honor's shoulders and steered her out of the bathroom. "Sweetie, go fix yourself up," she whispered. "You have lipstick on your teeth."

Closing the door, Karma winked at the bride. "Phew, I thought she'd never leave!"

Antoinette dropped onto the suede bench and dabbed at her eyes with her fingertips. "I don't know what to do," she said quietly, staring at her solitaire engagement ring.

"Every time you come by the salon you gush about how incredible your fiancé is, so why are you doubting his love and devotion now?"

Laughter and cheers rang out in the suite, and the music got louder.

"I'm scared, Karma. This is my second marriage. What if it doesn't work out? What if ten years down the line I end up getting another divorce? What then?"

Crouching down in front of the bench, Karma took Antoinette's hands in hers and squeezed them, wanting her to know she wasn't alone. "In life there are no guarantees, but—"

"Winston wants kids," Antoinette announced, cutting Karma off midsentence. "But what if I'm too old to conceive? What if my eggs have all shriveled up and died?"

"Have you talked to Winston about your fears?"

At the mention of her fiancé's name her eyes lit up, and her smile returned. "Yes, of course," she said, slowly nodding her head. "He said if we can't conceive naturally we'll adopt."

"You're right, Antoinette. He *is* a good man." To lighten the mood, Karma raised an eyebrow and joked, "And I wouldn't worry about conceiving naturally if I were you. Winston's going to take one look at you in your breathtaking, custom-made Pnina Tornai gown and drag you to the pastor's office for a quickie!"

A bridesmaid banged on the door. "Time to shake a leg, Antoinette. The photographer's here, and we can't afford to fall behind schedule…"

Antoinette didn't move.

"You're going to have the wedding of your dreams, and as long as you remember to keep the marriage commandments you'll have a long, prosperous and passionate union."

Antoinette raised her bent shoulders and rose to her feet. "The marriage commandments?" she repeated, dabbing at her cheeks with the sleeve of her robe. "What's that?"

"The rules every wife should live by, of course."

Interest sparked in her eyes. "I've never heard of it. What are they?"

Struggling to keep a straight face, Karma gripped Antoinette's shoulders, stared deep in her eyes and spoke in a stern voice. "Thou shalt love your husband, support your husband *and* rock his world in the bedroom *twice* every night!"

Antoinette tossed her head back and erupted in laughter.

The sound was music to Karma's ears. "Don't laugh too hard," she teased, wagging a finger in the bride's face. "You'll ruin your makeup, and I don't have time to redo it, so knock it off, Mrs. Winston Tolbert-to-be."

The women embraced, and Antoinette giggled again.

"Thanks for the laugh, Karma. I needed it."

Karma positioned Antoinette in front of the mirror, then stepped aside.

"Oh my goodness. What did you do? It doesn't even look like me!"

"Do you like it?" Karma held her breath, hoped she'd captured the bride's vision.

"I don't like it. I *love* it," she gushed, touching her fancy updo with her fingertips.

"Ready to marry your one true love?"

Antoinette eagerly nodded her head. "You bet your Louboutins I am. Let's do this!"

Karma sat inside the Mother African Methodist Episcopal Zion Church in Harlem, marveling at the beauty of the oldest black church in New York. The Gothic-style building was a historical landmark that was as grand as it was regal. Sunshine poured through the stained-glass windows, casting a halo around the bride and groom, and the air was perfumed with a sweet, fragrant scent. From the extravagant flower display, to the larger-than-life archway and celebrity pianist, it was obvious the couple had spared no expense planning their five-hundred-guest wedding. Pillars were swathed in red roses, vines and peonies, creating a garden-like effect, shiny, oversize bows hung from each pew, and potted candles lined the satin-draped aisle.

Opening her clutch purse, Karma retrieved her silk handkerchief and fanned her face. Listening to the groom recite his personalized wedding vows brought tears to her eyes and made her realize everything Antoinette had ever told her about Winston was true. His excitement was palpable, and the expression on his face was sincere. The female guests released a collective sigh as the CEO gazed longingly at his bride.

Karma considered her past relationships. No one had ever spoken to her with such warmth, such tenderness. *That's why I'm still single*, she thought with a heavy heart. *I'd rather be alone than settle for anything less than I de-*

serve. She'd never admit it to anyone, not even Jazz, but she was tired of being alone, and wanted one special man in her life who'd cherish her. Realizing she was getting caught up in the moment, Karma gave her head a shake and listened intently to what the minister was saying.

"Today, before all of us in this assembly, you have declared you will live together in holy matrimony and God is well pleased. You have made vows, and promises to each other, exchanged rings with hands joined in unity, and by the authority given to me as a minister in the state of New York, I now pronounce you husband and wife," he said, clapping the groom on the shoulder. "Winston, you may kiss your beautiful bride."

As the couple shared their first kiss as husband and wife, guests stood and applauded.

That's when Karma saw *him.* Morrison Drake. The nerve endings in her body stirred, then tingled. Taller than everyone else in the church, he was impossible to miss. She should have known Morrison would be at the Tolbert-Lefevre wedding. It was the social event of the year, one of the most lavish weddings Karma had ever been to, and although she couldn't see the president and the first lady from her corner seat, the minister had publicly acknowledged them.

Karma stepped out of the pew. To get a better look at Morrison, she peered around a heavyset gentleman in a tacky, orange suit, and stood on her tiptoes. To die for, in his black, velvet-trimmed suit jacket, it was no surprise the female guests in his pew were boldly checking him out. Was the brunette in the tight, peach dress his date? Or the slender Asian woman with the ridiculously long weave?

"Ladies and gentlemen, may I present to you, Mr. and Mrs. Winston Tolbert!"

Guests cheered, cameras flashed and Karma snapped to attention. Leaving the hotel that morning, Antoinette had told her once the ceremony started she was officially off the clock, and as the couple danced down the aisle to their favorite Celine Dion song Karma waved and whistled. Karma loved weddings, had a blast partying with her clients' friends and family, and when the bride's mother thanked her for saving the day, she beamed.

All around her, guests chatted and laughed, traded hugs and snapped pictures, but Karma kept a watchful eye on Morrison as he moved around the church. He was gruff and salty, but damn he was fine. His eyes, his mouth, his physique, his debonair vibe. Wetting her lips with her tongue, Karma admired his profile.

Morrison spotted her, staring at him, and time stopped. Surprise covered his face, and then a broad grin curled his lips. Never, in her life, had she desired a man more, and his deep, dark stare left her breathless. And horny. More aroused than a bachelorette at *Magic Mike Live*.

Karma looked on with interest, wondering what Judge Hottie was going to do next. Ending his conversation with a willowy blonde draped in diamonds, Morrison shouldered his way through the crowd and headed up the aisle—straight toward her! Their chemistry was powerful, all consuming and, even though he was across the room, she was trembling.

Glancing around, Karma searched for the nearest exit. The urge to run was so strong she wanted to kick off her floral-print satin pumps, hike up her designer gown and bolt through the church doors, but since she didn't want to plough into the newlyweds, who were posing for guests and photographers in the foyer, Karma waited patiently for them to finish.

Relax, relate, release, she chanted, resting a hand on

her midsection to still the butterflies swarming around her empty stomach. Leaving the Royal Suite, she'd grabbed a banana from the fruit bowl, but it didn't pacify her hunger, and once Karma congratulated the bride and groom she was heading to the nearest burger joint.

"You weren't going to leave without saying hi, were you?" Morrison leaned in close and kissed her cheek. "How do you know the happy couple?"

"I used to do Antoinette's hair when she lived in the Hamptons, so when she called and asked me to do her hair and makeup for her big day I said, 'hell yeah!'"

Morrison whistled. "Wow, I'm impressed. I've never seen her look so glamorous."

"I think her custom-made gown had something to do with it, but thanks," Karma said with a laugh, glancing over her shoulder at the bride. "I take great pride in what I do, and making my clients happy is my number one priority, so I always try my best to capture their vision."

Her heart was beating a million miles a second, but she maintained her poise.

"I almost didn't recognize you," he said. "You look so different with braids."

Taken aback by his words, she raised an eyebrow. "Different bad, or different good?"

"The latter of course. You're stunning, Karma, simply and utterly captivating," he praised, in an appreciative tone of voice. "Hell, you're so fine you'd look good with a mullet!"

Karma laughed long and hard, couldn't believe how funny he was. Bored with her hair, she'd braided it last night in Senegalese twists. For the wedding, she'd piled them on top of her head in an elegant bun, and diamond clips added a touch of glamour. All day, she'd been receiving compliments, and at the start of the ceremony five women had booked her on the spot to get their hair done at Beauty by Karma. Her schedule was already jam-packed, filled with dozens of back-to-back appointments next week, but Karma had entered the slots in her cell phone calendar and emailed it to Abigail.

Karma pinned her shoulders back and straightened her spine. She smoothed a hand over her hips, then adjusted the diamond choker at her neck. Her satin Balenciaga gown had cost a small fortune, but once she'd tried it on at the by-appointment-only boutique in Southampton, she was in love. It accentuated her best features, hid her flaws and the vibrant teal shade made her eyes pop. Jazz had insisted she buy it as an early birthday present to herself, and Karma was glad she'd listened to her bestie. Her nerves were out of whack, and perspiration wet her skin but she'd never felt more beautiful.

"That dress was made for you, and the color complements your complexion perfectly."

Transfixed by the sound of his voice, and his distinct, masculine scent, Karma didn't speak. Someone bumped into her from behind, pushing her into his chest, and heat flooded her skin. "Sorry about that," she murmured, regaining her balance. "Someone pushed me."

"No problem. I like holding beautiful women in my arms."

"What's gotten into you? You're giving out compliments like they're candy," Karma teased, shocked that this was the same man who'd insulted her last Saturday at her beauty salon. She couldn't wrap her brain around it, couldn't figure out why Morrison was being so nice to her. Had Reagan put him up to this? Was he trying to make amends for barging into Beauty by Karma last weekend and causing a scene?

"You're right. I better stop flirting with you before

your date beats me up." He gestured at the well-dressed crowd mingling in the church, and said, "Where is he? I'd love to meet him."

"I don't have a date. I'm here alone."

"Great, then you can be my plus one at the reception."

"*You* don't have a date?"

Mischief filled his eyes. "I do now. *You.*"

"Your family isn't here with you tonight?"

"My brothers were supposed to drive down with me last night, but Duane's youngest son is sick with pneumonia, and he didn't want to leave him," Morrison explained. "And Roderick's fiancée surprised him with a weekend getaway to Cabo, so I'm flying solo tonight."

Karma swallowed hard. Morrison was just inches away from her, close enough to kiss, to touch, but she resisted the needs of her flesh. Had to, or she'd embarrass herself. Morrison was a powerful, successful man who probably thought women should be seen, not heard, and Karma didn't want to hook up with someone who didn't respect her—no matter how dreamy he was.

"It's settled. We'll sit together at the reception, and you can tell me more about your—"

Interrupting him, she fervently shook her head. "Morrison, I can't. There are table assignments, and place cards, and I don't want to mess up Antoinette's seating chart."

"Don't worry, beautiful. I've got this. Leave everything to me."

He lowered his mouth to her ear, and Karma shivered. Why did that keep happening? Why did her limbs shake, and her knees wobble every time he looked at her? It didn't matter how many times she tried, she couldn't speak.

Placing a hand on her back, he led her out of the

church and across the street to where his sleek, black Bentley was parked. Watching him on the sly, Karma didn't know if she should be mad at his take-charge attitude or impressed. But as Morrison gently caressed her shoulders and hips, desire—not anger—shot through her veins, and Karma knew if she wasn't careful she'd be another notch on his belt, and there was no way in hell she'd ever let that happen.

Chapter 6

Over the years, Karma had been to dozens of black-tie dinners and high-profile events in New York, but nothing compared to the Tolbert-Lefevre wedding. It was a lavish, over-the-top affair that had it all: a dramatic entrance with flame throwers, a scrumptious, seven-course meal prepared by a celebrity master chef, an energetic emcee who made guests laugh out loud, and a surprise performance from the Queen of Hip-Hop and Soul.

Raising her flute to her lips, Karma spotted belly dancers waiting outside the ballroom doors and admired their colorful costumes. The Tolbert-Lefevre reception wasn't a party; it was a Hollywood production, with more A-list stars than the Grammys, and Karma was having the time of her life. She'd met the mayor, taken a selfie with a Spice Girl and blogged about the wedding from the comfort of her satin-draped chair.

Hanging lanterns, ivory-adorned centerpieces, rose-gold candlesticks and round tables dressed in fine china created a whimsical, romantic decor in the Four Seasons grand ballroom. The elaborate candy station, with the three-tier fondue fountain, had long lines, but Karma liked the black-and-white photo booth the best. She'd never taken so many photographs in her life, but every time Morrison suggested they take one more she struck a pose.

From the time they'd arrived at the grand ballroom, Karma and Morrison had been talking, flirting and cracking jokes. They'd been sitting at Table Nine for hours, chatting about their careers, mutual friends and acquaintances, and their favorite hangout spots in the city. Morrison had an opinion about everything, but his sense of humor was his most endearing quality. Witty and self-deprecating, he made Karma laugh until tears spilled down her cheeks. And she wasn't the only one. They were sitting with four other couples, and the women at the table were giggling too. Morrison was telling the group about his trip to Asia months earlier, and everyone was hanging on to his every word—even the pretentious plastic surgeon and his decades-younger wife.

"Tokyo and Hong Kong are fantastic cities, with incredibly kind and gracious people, but Singapore was by far my favorite country to visit."

"Really? Why?" questioned the female biochemist. "What made it stand out for you?"

Cocking an eyebrow, Morrison pulled back the sleeve of his shirt and tapped the face of his gold, Gucci wristwatch. "How much time do you have because once I start talking about my travels there's just no stopping me!"

The women tittered, the men chuckled, and Karma propped her face up in her hands. She could listen to Morrison talk all night, would never tire of his charm, his wit and his smooth-as-silk baritone. The belly dancers burst into the room, eliciting a cheer from the guests, but Karma didn't take her eyes off Judge Hottie. Conversation was put on hold, but once the dancers finished their routine, Morrison finished his story.

"Singapore is a city, and an island, and a country all in one, and every day was an exciting, new adventure," he explained, picking up his water glass. "I tried zip lining for the first time, had breakfast with the orangutans at the Singapore Zoo, enjoyed a private sightseeing tour through the city at sunrise, and I made several good friends along the way, as well…"

Female friends? Karma wondered, jealousy rearing its ugly head.

Of course *they're women*, quipped her inner voice. *Look at him! He's tall, debonair and dreamy, and if you weren't afraid of getting hurt you'd do him in a New York minute!*

"Give a round of applause to Mr. and Mrs. Winston Tolbert," the emcee shouted.

Popping another chocolate raspberry truffle into her mouth, Karma watched with rapt attention as the bride and groom approached the raised podium. Remembering her favorite moment of the night, she laughed to herself. After dessert, Antoinette had ordered all of the single women to the dance floor, but when Karma saw the tulip-filled bouquet flying toward her she'd jumped out of the way. Morrison hadn't been so lucky, but chuckled good-naturedly when the black, lace garter landed at his feet. Much to the crowd's delight, he'd scooped it up in his hands, waved it in the air, then danced back to his seat. Women whistled, swooned and cheered. Of course. It didn't surprise her. Morrison was the most eligible bachelor in the Hamptons and couldn't go anywhere without females ogling him, and Manhattan was no different.

"Today I married my best friend, my one true love, and I want to thank everyone in this room for helping me make my dreams come true," Antoinette said, snuggling against her new husband. "We are humbled by your unwavering support, and we wouldn't be the couple we are today without each and every one of you cheering us on. My husband is the greatest gift I've ever been given, and every time he kisses me I feel like the luckiest woman alive…"

Karma admired the bride's poise and eloquence. Twelve hours ago, Antoinette had been panicking, and now she was grinning at her husband, so blissfully in love stars shimmered in her eyes. Karma thought she'd seen it all, couldn't imagine anything more heartwarming than the couple's first dance, but their poignant thank-you speech moved her to tears.

"Now, it's time to get down and dirty, so get out of your seats, and let's hit the dance floor!" Winston shouted, pumping his fist in the air to the beat of the hip-hop song playing in the background. "Come on, baby, let's show them how it's done…"

Eager to bust a move, everyone at Table Nine jumped up from their seats, but Karma didn't move. Her expensive designer pumps were made for walking, not bumping and grinding, and since she didn't want to roll her ankle on the eve of her thirtieth birthday Karma stayed put. She crossed her legs and sipped her cocktail as her tablemates waved goodbye.

"You're not coming? But they're playing the 'Cha Cha Slide.' It's a classic." Standing, Morrison loosened the knot in his black tie, took off his suit jacket and draped it behind his chair. "You have to come. It's going to be fun."

"Maybe later," she said, pretending not to notice the disappointment in his eyes. "I'm going to sit this one out, but you go ahead. Shake a leg for the both of us, Judge Drake!"

Chuckling, he dropped his mouth to her ear and a hand to her thigh. His cologne washed over her, the spicy, sandalwood scent so enticing her mouth was moist. "Sit tight, beautiful. I'll be back in a few, so don't go anywhere."

Morrison kissed her cheek, then turned and marched through the room. But he didn't make it. Besieged by an army of perky, twentysomething women with lust in their eyes, he stopped abruptly and flashed a smile. As if under a trance, they followed him toward the dance floor, snapping their fingers and swiveling their hips. The crowd parted when Morrison arrived, and from the front of the grand ballroom, he led the group in the steps of the Cha Cha Slide. Amazed, and impressed, Karma straightened in her chair. She'd never seen a man move like that before, let alone a judge, and wondered what other skills Morrison had. *Does he move like that in the bedroom? Is he a passionate and selfless lover?*

Karma picked up her glass and finished the rest of her drink. The sweet liquid quenched her thirst, helped to cool the raging fire in her body. Her eyes were glued to Morrison, boldly admired him. With his energy and charisma, he garnered more attention than a presidential Tweet, and owned the heart of every woman in the room. Morrison danced to so many songs, with so many different guests, Karma marveled at his stamina. Shrieked and cheered when he did the splits. Morrison knew all of the latest dances, and moved his body with ease and confidence, seemed to feed off the excitement in the air as he joined the *Soul Train* line.

Checking the time on her cell, Karma grabbed her purse, tucked it under her arm and rose to her feet. She'd had a blast at the Tolbert-Lefevre wedding, but she wanted to return to her suite to freshen up before

Jazz arrived, and she hurried to say good-night to the bride and groom. Several hugs and kisses later, Karma sashayed out the ballroom doors, and into the bright, grandiose lobby. The crystal chandeliers, designer furniture and eclectic wall paintings screamed of glamour, and added to the serene ambiance of the posh hotel.

"One minute, you're sitting pretty at the table nursing a virgin margarita, and the next thing I know you're running off. What gives, Karma? I thought we were having a good time?"

At the sound of Morrison's voice, she glanced over her shoulder, ready to fire off a witty retort, but when their eyes locked the quip died on her lips. Karma didn't think it was possible for Morrison to look any sexier, but his shirt sleeves were rolled up, and his boyish grin gave him an edge, a bad-boy vibe she found irresistible. Drenched in sweat, his designer threads clung to his biceps and chest, and the bulge in his pants was pronounced. Eye-catching, and arousing. Something Karma's wayward hands were itching to stroke and caress—

"Come back inside," Morrison said, touching her forearm. "I want to dance with you."

He wore a hopeful look on his face, and if Karma didn't have plans with Jazz tonight she'd return to the grand ballroom. Morrison had surprised her at the reception, had proved that he wasn't the stuffy, uptight judge she'd thought he was, and he was great company.

"I can't dance with you. You're way out of my league," she teased him. "You're wasting your talents behind the bench, Mr. Drake. You're such a talented dancer, you should be a Jabbawockeez!"

Morrison chuckled, and his hearty belly laugh made Karma giggle.

"I wish I could stay, but my best friend should be here

any minute and I want to freshen up before we head out for some late-night fun in the city."

"I understand. Just let me grab my jacket, and I'll walk you to your suite."

Before Karma could protest, Morrison jogged back down the hall and into the grand ballroom to retrieve his things. To kill time, Karma, took her cell out of her purse and accessed her email. She had several messages from her attorney regarding the business expansion project, and reading them made her smile. If everything went according to plan, she'd have three more locations for her salon next year, and with the help of her team, shops worldwide.

"Ready to shake a leg?" Morrison asked, resting a hand on her shoulder.

Walking through the lobby, everyone they passed smiled and waved at Morrison, shaking his hand with gusto. He was the kind of man every woman wanted to bring home to their parents, but when Karma teased him about being popular he played it off.

"Not me, per se, but my dad. He has lots of friends and business associates in the city, and they just want to extend their well wishes to my father."

"Is he ill?"

"No. He had hip surgery three months ago, and his recovery has been a long, slow process."

"It's hard seeing the people you love suffer with health issues," Karma said with a sympathetic smile. "My grandparents are in their eighties, and struggling as they age, as well. Thankfully, I found a retired nurse to provide live-in care at their home, and now they're doing much better. Hopefully, it stays that way."

Morrison whistled. "Twenty-four-hour care? Wow, that must be expensive."

"It is, but nothing matters more to me than taking care of my grandparents. They've been my rock since my parents died, and I cherish our weekly visits. They're a riot!"

Boarding the elevator, Karma heard her Lady Gaga ring tone, and broke into a smile. She couldn't wait to see Jazz, was anxious to tell her about the Tolbert-Lefevre wedding, her conversations with Morrison at the reception, and all the flirting and touching they'd done.

"Hey, Jazz, what's up?" she greeted, leaning against the wall. Karma wanted to kick off her shoes, and rub her aching feet, but since she didn't want Morrison to think she was ghetto, she ignored the searing pain in her toes and spoke to Jazz. "Where are you? Almost here?"

"Karma, I have good news and bad news. Which one do you want to hear first?"

Excitement and dread flooded her stomach in equal measurers. "The good news."

"Platinum Dolls booked us to do their hair and makeup for their music video in Barbados on Friday, and yours truly got us parts. We're going to be extras! "

"Wow, Jazz, that's great! Way to go!" Karma laughed. "Hollywood, here we come!"

"I know, right? I'm so hyped I feel like shouting from the rooftops."

"Me too, so wait until you get here, and we'll do it together—"

"About that," Jazz said quietly, her voice tinged with apprehension. "Lorenzo surprised me with a romantic weekend on his yacht, so I won't be coming to the city."

"Ha-ha, very funny. Quit playing."

"We'll celebrate when I get back. I promise."

The elevator doors slid open, and Karma forced her legs to move. Noticing the worried expression on Morrison's face, she wore a weak smile and searched the hall for her suite. "But tomorrow's my birthday, and you promised we'd celebrate *big*."

"And we will. We'll throw a party at the salon on Monday, and—"

"Monday?" Karma repeated, rolling her eyes. "Why bother? Jazz, just forget it."

"Don't be like that. You know I'd come to the city if I could."

Karma opened her mouth, realized she was at a loss for words, and closed it. She couldn't believe what Jazz had said, couldn't believe her bestie was dissing her to hook up with a wealthy Spaniard she'd met a week earlier at the gym. A month ago, she'd taken three days off work to celebrate Jazz's twenty-eighth birthday in Las Vegas, and had spared no expense. While being pampered at the resort spa, Jazz had admitted it was the best birthday she'd ever had, and promised to make Karma's thirtieth birthday memorable. *What am I going to do now?* Karma couldn't think of anything more depressing than spending her thirtieth birthday alone, but she gathered herself, and said, "Whatever, Jazz. Don't worry about me. I'll be fine. Have fun with your boyfriend."

"I don't understand why you're so upset," Jazz snapped back. "You canceled on me first."

"I didn't cancel on you. I adjusted my schedule because I had to work, not because I took off with some dude I barely know for the weekend."

Silence infected the line, and when the dial tone buzzed in her ear Karma knew she'd gone too far. The right thing to do was to call Jazz back and apologize, but her pride wouldn't let her. Hurt and upset, Karma wanted to go to her room and raid the minibar, not argue with her bestie about her misplaced loyalty.

"We've been hanging out for hours, but you never

mentioned your birthday was tomorrow," Morrison said, giving her a one-arm hug. "What are your plans?"

"I don't have any. My best friend was supposed to meet me here, so we could spend tomorrow in the city, but she got a better offer so I'm on my own."

"No, you're not. I'll spend the day with you."

Giving him a funny look, Karma stopped in front of her suite door. "Sure you will."

"I'm serious. Reagan's with my parents, and my brothers are busy with their families this weekend so there's no reason to rush home," he said, sliding a hand into his pants pocket. "So, what's on the itinerary, Birthday Girl? Shopping, fine dining, a stage play or dancing?"

"All of the above!"

Morrison laughed, and a smile overwhelmed Karma's lips. She never would have guessed, not in a million years, that she'd be spending her thirtieth birthday with Morrison Drake. Karma didn't think they'd have anything in common, but during the reception she discovered they both loved board games, reggae music and horror movies. To her relief, Morrison wasn't a stick-in-the-mud. A New Yorker through and through, he was sociable and sarcastic, and joked good-naturedly about his brothers, his colleagues at the courthouse and his ever-growing bucket list. "I'm going to sleep in tomorrow, so let's meet in the lobby at ten o'clock."

"Thankfully, I'm just down the hall, so I'll come get you in the morning."

"Sounds like a plan," Karma said brightly, digging around in her purse for her key card. Unable to find it, she took everything out of the pocket, but still came up empty. Shaking her head in frustration, her shoulders drooped. "Oh great, I lost my room key."

"Don't sweat it. You can call the front desk from my suite and request another one."

"Thanks," she said with a sheepish smile, hoping he didn't think she was a ditz. "That would be great. I'm beat, and I don't feel like going all the way back downstairs."

Morrison led the way, and she followed him to the room at the end of the hall. Entering the spacious suite filled with attractive furnishings, pendant lamps and plush, cream-colored carpet, Karma noticed the space was spotless and suspected Judge Hottie was a neat freak.

Examining his profile in detail, her mouth dried and her heart fluttered. With his low-cut hair, studious demeanour and chiseled body, Morrison could be the poster boy for the US Marines. Remembering she was there to use the phone, not lust after him, Karma broke free of her thoughts and approached the Brazilian walnut desk. Polite and sympathetic, the front-desk clerk promised to send the concierge up with another key, and Karma ended the call.

"Do you want me to fix you a drink while you wait?"

I'm thirsty, but not for champagne.

Morrison gestured to the stainless steel fridge in the gourmet kitchen. "I can't make a margarita, but I make a mean rum and Coke if you're interested."

"No, thanks. The concierge will be here shortly."

Reaching out, he coiled his index finger around the stray twist that had escaped her bun. "I like your hair in braids. It makes you look regal, like African royalty."

"Why thank you, Mr. Drake."

His eyes dimmed. "I like it better when you call me Morrison."

"What else do you like?"

Bracing his hands against the door, fencing her in,

Morrison stared intently at her, his gaze smouldering with desire. Inwardly chastising herself for her salacious quip, Karma sucked in a breath. *Why did I say that? Why am I flirting with a man who is totally out of my league?* Her loose lips had gotten her into trouble, and the longer he stared at her the harder her limbs shook. Her head was spinning, but she projected confidence, not fear, and said, "Thank you for a wonderful evening, Morrison. Good night."

"It's midnight," he announced, lowering his mouth to her face. "Happy Birthday, beautiful. I hope this year brings prosperity, excitement and adventure. They don't call it the Dirty Thirties for nothing, so throw caution to the wind and own every moment."

Shivering as his lips moved gently against hers, she willed her legs not to buckle. Deep down, she craved his touch, his kiss, but she wasn't brave enough to make the first move.

"Life is not remembered in days, Karma. It is remembered in moments, and this moment will remain with me forever."

Catching her off guard, Morrison pulled her to his chest with one hand, cupped her cheek with the other, and kissed her with such passion and desperation, Karma gasped. She moaned inside his mouth, over and over again, couldn't stop from voicing her pleasure. It was one kiss. No big deal. Nothing to feel guilty about, she told herself, feasting on his juicy lips. It was her thirtieth birthday, and since Karma couldn't think of anything better than making out for a few minutes with a dashing, debonair man, she draped her arms around his neck and deepened the kiss. Wanted to show Morrison just how much she desired him.

His mouth was relentless in its pursuit, sucking, teasing, licking, taking everything she had to give and more. Lost in the moment, Karma didn't have the strength to break free, couldn't end the kiss if her life depended on it. Karma struggled to breathe, couldn't catch her breath. Goose bumps flooded her skin, and butterflies danced in her stomach. She wanted to tell Morrison to stop, knew she should leave his suite before they crossed the line, but the words didn't come. Got stuck in her throat. Moans fell from her lips instead. And, when Morrison sprayed soft kisses against her neck, and slid a hand under her dress, Karma knew they'd reached the point of no return.

Chapter 7

A sensation came over Morrison—strong, powerful urges he'd never experienced before. Desires he couldn't ignore or control. In that moment, nothing mattered more to him than kissing Karma, so he did. Took her arms, pinned them above her head and devoured her moist, plump lips. He expected her to pull away, but she surprised him by inclining her head. Karma moaned inside his mouth, licked and teased his tongue, boldly stroked his chest through his clothes, and Morrison loved every minute of it.

The kiss exceeded his expectations, and Morrison wanted more. Sliding his tongue past her teeth, he probed her warm mouth, reveled in their closeness, their first kiss. Unlike his friends, and brothers, he'd never had a one-night stand or a friend with benefits, but Karma made him act out of character and thoughts of making love to her dominated his mind. Hanging out with her at the reception, it was easy to see why everyone adored her. Karma had moxie, an infectious laugh and personality, and her tell-it-like-it-is outlook on life was refreshing. She enjoyed flirting and cracking jokes, and even though every time he turned around someone was putting the moves on her—a city councilman, an NBA superstar, a Latin actor oozing with charm—he'd kept his head, didn't trip when other men made a play for her.

"Damn, you taste good. Like champagne. My favorite."

"I can't believe we're making out in your suite," she confessed. "I thought you were a serious, no-nonsense judge who didn't know how to have fun."

"Spend the night, and I'll show you just how *fun* I can be."

He kissed her hard on the mouth, allowed his lips to linger against hers, tenderly stroked her shoulders and hips. Karma guided his hands to her breasts, and rubbed her hips against his crotch. All night the excitement had been building, and now the scent of their desire consumed his suite. Karma had the sexual confidence of a nude model, moved her body in such an erotic way his mouth dried, and his erection strained against the zipper of his tailored, suit pants. His patience had paid off, and now he was kissing the most desirable woman he'd ever met. He was losing it, grunting and groaning, and Karma was the reason why. Her dress was in his way. Annoying him. Morrison wanted to rip it from her body, bend her over the chocolate-brown couch and thrust inside her, but exercised self-control.

Morrison gazed down at her. He saw apprehension in her eyes and wondered if Karma was having second thoughts about spending the night with him. Sometimes doing the right thing sucked, so instead of kissing her again, he said, "We should stop before we cross the line."

"We already did." Karma trailed her tongue along his lips, flicked it against his teeth. "You're not trying to talk me out of making love *after* you made me wet, are you?

I hope not, because it's my birthday, and you should be spoiling me, not rejecting me."

He grinned. "I wouldn't dream of it."

"This is crazy. You hate me, and think I'm a bad influence on your niece—"

"Don't say that. I don't hate you. I think you erred in judgment hiring Reagan to work at your salon, but it's obvious you care about her, and I'm glad she feels comfortable talking to you about her problems."

"Morrison, stop, I own a beauty salon, not a strip club," she snapped back. "There's nothing nefarious happening at Beauty by Karma and we don't talk about anything Reagan hasn't already heard on MTV or social media. In fact, *she's* the one schooling us!"

Morrison didn't like the sound of that, wanted to know exactly what his teenage niece was up to, but when he pressed her for details she fervently shook her head. "Sorry, Morrison, no can do. What happens at Beauty by Karma, stays at Beauty by Karma."

"We'll see about that," he murmured against her mouth in a husky tone of voice, nibbling on the corner of her lips. "I'm sure there's *something* I can do to change your mind."

"Or not," she quipped. "I have nerves of steel."

Morrison unzipped her dress, then helped her out of it. He slid his hands along her hips, caressing her warm flesh. Sexy in a black lace bra and thong panties, he marveled at her curvy shape. He pressed his mouth against her ears, her neck and shoulders, licked and tasted her skin with his tongue.

Morrison heard a loud knock on the suite door, knew the concierge had arrived with a spare room key, but decided it would have to wait. Nothing mattered more to him than pleasing Karma, and he didn't want anything to ruin the moment.

Facing him, Karma unhooked her bra, tossed it onto the couch and cupped her breasts in her hands. Morrison felt his eyes widen and his jaw drop. The silver chain around her neck was attached to a nipple ring, and watching Karma play with her nipples was the most erotic thing he'd ever seen. He wanted to touch her, to replace her hands with his own, but wanted the green light first. "Does it hurt?" he asked, gesturing to the metal nipple ring.

"It did when I first got it done, but not anymore. My girlfriends suggested we get piercings during our last girls' trip to Vegas, and I'm glad I did. My nipples are more sensitive now, and I instantly get aroused when I touch them."

Morrison moved closer to her. "Do you like it being tugged on? Can I suck it?"

"You're the first one trying it out, so to speak, but that sounds hot."

"Wow, you sure know how to make a guy feel special."

Taking her hand, he led her into the bedroom, and sat down on the king-size bed. Karma climbed onto his lap, and he sucked a nipple into his mouth, couldn't wait to explore her body. He took the ruffled elastic band out of her hair, and her braids fell around her shoulders and down her back. Using his tongue, he gently tugged on the ring, licked it, sucked it, pressed soft kisses around her breasts. Karma tossed her head back, rocked against him as his fingers caressed her hips and thighs, slowly circled and rubbed her navel.

Kissing him hard on the mouth, Karma ripped the designer shirt from his body, took off his pants and tossed them over her shoulder as if they were rags. She stroked his erection through his boxer briefs, and Morrison feared he was going to explode in her soft, delicate hands. Karma took the reins in the bedroom, and it was damn hot. She wasn't afraid to tell him what she wanted, what she needed, and it was a turn-on. Her compliments and praise made him feel as virile as a Roman gladiator, caused delicious shudders to rock his body.

"You make me feel sooo good," she purred. "I can't wait to feel you inside me…"

Hearing her talk dirty in bed excited him, and her words tipped him over the edge. Made him lose it. Forget the cardinal rule of dating. Morrison flipped Karma onto her back, hiked her legs in the air and entered her in one fluid motion. Grabbing her ankles, he deepened his thrusts, pumped and moved his hips in a circle. To please her, he cupped and squeezed her big, perky breasts. Her hands caressed his face, played in his hair, roughly tweaked his nipples and kneaded his biceps.

Tingles stabbed his spine. It drove Morrison crazy when Karma pulled him even deeper inside her sex, holding him in place with her hands. It was the pièce de résistance, the bold, erotic move that sent him hurtling back down to earth. Blood rushed to his head. Every nerve ending came to life, and his senses were razor sharp. He didn't want to stop, wanted to give Karma the best sex of her life, but he rode her hard and fast, welcoming the explosion that rocked his body. She clenched her pelvic muscles, and adrenaline shot through his veins, giving him a mind-blowing rush.

Arching his back, Morrison could feel himself losing control, falling victim to his needs. He collapsed on the bed, sweating and panting, and needed a moment to catch his breath. His eyes fell across the clock on the end table, and Morrison cringed. He was mad at himself for finishing so fast, but it wasn't his fault. He hadn't been intimate with anyone in months, but now that he'd had his appetizer he was ready for the main course. Though, the next time they had sex he'd make sure he used a condom. The one in his wallet wasn't going to be enough. He'd have to run down to the hotel gift shop and buy a box of Magnums, because now that he'd made love to Karma he wanted to do it again and again and again. Morrison opened his mouth to apologize for not using protection, but her fingertips grazed his nipples and he lost his train of thought.

"Wow," Karma rasped in an awe-filled voice. "Happy birthday to me, indeed!"

"No regrets?"

"None whatsoever. You?"

To put her mind at ease, Morrison draped an arm around her shoulder and kissed her forehead, the tip of her nose and finally her mouth. "How can I regret making love to a passionate, amorous woman who gave me the best sex of my life?"

Grinning, Karma rested her head on his chest and snuggled against him. Sweaty and thirsty, Morrison wanted a shower, and a cold beer from the minibar. Normally, he didn't indulge in pillow talk or cuddling, could think of a hundred things he'd rather do with his time than bare his soul, but he surprised himself by doing both with Karma. Their conversation was genuine, not forced or awkward, and full of laughs. His interest peaked when their discussion turned to relationships. Karma confided in him about her dreadful dating history, and soon Morrison was opening up to her about his ex-girlfriends. Their playful banter made him feel close to her, and as Karma giggled at his jokes his desire for her grew.

"What a day. I'm beat." Yawning, he closed his eyes

and stretched his neck from side to side. He'd been up since 5 a.m., but Morrison was so relaxed and content holding Karma in his arms he knew he'd sleep like a baby tonight. "I was going to grab something to eat from the minibar, but maybe I should call room service instead—"

"I should go." Karma struggled to sit up. "I'd hate to overstay my welcome."

"You're not going anywhere. We still have a lot of celebrating to do." Morrison pulled her into his arms. "Are you still mad at your best friend for bailing on you tonight?"

"Who?" she quipped, making her eyes wide. "I've been too busy having fun with you to give her a second thought, and I don't plan to."

"I'm glad to hear that. My thirtieth birthday was a disaster, and—"

Surprise filled her eyes. "It was? What happened? I want all the scandalous details."

"It's not going to happen. You'll laugh at me, and my ego's been bruised enough."

"I won't. I promise." Karma held up a finger. "Pinkie swear."

Morrison chuckled when she hooked his finger with hers and vowed to keep her word. He heard his cell ringing inside the living room, but he was too comfortable to move. Didn't want to interrupt his conversation with Karma by yapping on the phone. He knew from the jazz song playing that his mother was the one blowing up his cell, but since nothing said mama's boy like answering a post-sex call from Mom he made a mental note to text her later.

"What did you do? Did you party with your brothers? Where did you go?"

Morrison pried his lips apart. "The New York Bridal Expo."

Her eyebrows shot up, and she stared at him as if he was speaking pig latin. Morrison knew Karma was trying hard not to laugh, and wore a wry smile. He didn't blame her. His brothers had teased him mercilessly when they saw the pictures of him on social media, and to this day they still made fun of him for attending the bridal expo.

"Were you drugged and taken there against your will?"

Chuckling, he swatted her ass. "Stop teasing me or I'll take you over my knee."

"Another birthday present? Let's do it!"

Karma laughed, but before Morrison could make good on his threat, she propped her head up in her hands, and questioned him about the bridal expo, wanted to know how he ended up at the popular event and who he'd attended it with.

"The marketing executive I was dating at the time shared my birthday, so when she asked me to spend the day with her, and her mother who was visiting from Savannah, I agreed. Big mistake. I've never heard so much crying or squealing in my life, and every time I hear the 'Wedding March' I have flashbacks of my birthday from hell."

"You're a good man, Morrison. Your parents obviously raised you well."

"They did, but I'm not perfect. I mess up and make mistakes, like tonight with you."

Confusion marred her features. "What are you talking about?" she said, resting a hand on his cheek. "Our lovemaking was sensational. Incredible. Out of this world…"

"Everything happened so fast I didn't have time to grab a condom, and I feel like an ass for being irresponsible." Wearing an apologetic smile, he read the question in her eyes and put her fears to rest. "But you have nothing to worry about. I've never had unprotected sex, or an STD, and I get tested regularly."

"So do I, and I'm on birth control, but next time we make love we should definitely use a condom. You can never be too safe. I love kids, but I don't want to be anyone's mama…"

Distracted by the feel of her naked body against his, it was hard for Morrison to concentrate on what Karma was saying, but he raised his gaze from her breasts to her eyes, and stopped fantasizing about making love to her in the marble-and-glass shower.

"Next time, huh?" Morrison wiggled his eyebrows. "Any guess when that will be?"

"That depends on how long you need to recharge."

"I don't." Standing, he searched the carpet for his pants, spotted them in front of the walk-in closet and retrieved his wallet. Morrison found the condom, opened it and covered his erection. "I'm ready when you are," he announced, rejoining her on the bed.

Climbing on top of him so her head was facing his feet, Karma sucked his erection into her open mouth, sucking it as if it was a Popsicle and she was starving. She cupped his shaft with her breasts, vigorously slid them up and down, panting and moaning. His eyes rolled in the back of his head. He wanted her to stop, knew he'd lose it again if she continued flicking her tongue against his shaft, but Morrison had no words. Couldn't get his lips to move.

Pleasure flooded his body, filling him to the brim, but he surfaced from his sexual haze and trailed his tongue along her tailbone. He kissed it, licked it, pressed his mouth against the fleshy lips between her thighs.

Crying out, she squirmed and rocked against him. Mounting him, she kissed him passionately on the lips, then pumped her hips like a horse jockey riding a Thoroughbred. *"Sí, cariño, dame más,"* she shouted, tossing her head back.

Morrison cupped her breasts, reverently kissed and sucked each nipple, nipped at it with his teeth. His chest inflated with pride, and his erection grew inside her, doubled in length. He'd never been with a woman who was so vocal, or amorous in the bedroom, and when she started talking dirty in Spanish, his mouth became wet. Karma was his newest obsession, a living fantasy, and Morrison wasn't letting the sultry stylist out of his sight for the rest of the weekend.

Chapter 8

Sunshine, powder blue skies and the warm breeze blowing through Manhattan made Karma feel relaxed and content, and when Morrison clasped her hand and led her through the front doors of the Four Seasons Hotel on Sunday afternoon her heart soared to the heavens.

Erotic images overwhelmed Karma's mind, and a smile curled her lips. Last night, after a quickie in the shower, they'd raided the minibar and collapsed onto the couch to eat. For hours, they'd talked and laughed and kissed. By the time Morrison went down to the front desk to get Karma's new key card and escorted her back to her suite the sun was climbing over the horizon.

Six hours later, Karma was *still* walking on air. That morning, they'd gone to the hotel restaurant for their legendary buffet brunch, and bumped into several guests from the Tolbert-Lefevre wedding. Joining the large, energetic group, they'd chatted about the highlights of the reception and their plans for the day. Morrison had let it slip that it was Karma's thirtieth birthday, then led the group in singing her "Happy Birthday." Draping an arm around her chair, he'd held her close as he fed her fruit-topped cheesecake. Wanting to look great but comfortable as they spent the day strolling around the city, Karma had paired her pink minidress with a floral bomber jacket, bejeweled sandals and silver accessories. She'd worn her braids down, and from the time they left the restaurant Morrison had been showering her with compliments.

The suit-clad driver, with eyeglasses and Albert Einstein hair, was standing in front of the limousine parked at the curb and bowed at the waist. "Happy birthday, Ms. Sullivan."

Surprised, Karma closed her gaping mouth and glanced at Morrison. "What's this?"

"Your wheels for the day. You deserve to be spoiled, so get in."

"But we agreed to walk to the museum—"

Morrison dropped his mouth to her ear and brushed his lips against it. "That was *before* you had your way with me in the shower," he whispered, in a silky-smooth voice. "After round three, my legs felt like rubber, so I called the best luxury car rental company in the city first thing this morning and booked a limousine for the day."

Karma gave him a peck on the lips. "I've always dreamed of making love in a limo."

"And today, I'm going to make sure all of your dreams come true."

The driver took her overnight bag, then opened the back door and stepped aside. Smiling her thanks, she inhaled the piquant aromas in the air. Inside the limousine were thirty helium balloons, a bouquet of colored roses, an oversize gift bag and a diamond tiara. Taking the seat beside her, Morrison placed the tiara on her head, then pressed his lips to her mouth.

"*Now* you're ready to party," he teased.

"Thanks for everything, Morrison. I'm having an incredible birthday."

"And it's about to get even better. Open your present."

"You didn't have to buy me anything. You've already done enough."

"My motto is go big or go home, and I knocked it out of the park."

"I love your humility," Karma joked, making a silly face. "It's *so* endearing."

The limousine pulled away from the curb and cruised through Midtown, passing trendy shops, restaurants and art galleries. Joggers, dog lovers and tourists crowded the sidewalks, and a steady stream of shoppers flowed in and out of upscale boutiques. Her hometown was full of delicious food, eccentric people, breathtaking sights and endless things to see and do, and as she gazed at the stately buildings and skyscrapers Karma smiled to herself. Was grateful to be in the greatest city in the world, living life on her terms.

"Come on," he drawled, leaning forward in his seat. "The suspense is killing me."

Karma reached into the bag, took out the pink envelope and ripped it open. The card played music, a popular song from the '90s by Janet Jackson, and she laughed out loud as she read the handwritten note Morrison had scrawled inside.

Happy Birthday to the sexiest woman in New York.
I'd go anywhere with you, even a bridal show, but please don't make me!
From your birthday bae,
Morrison Drake

"Like it?" he asked, his eyes bright with mischief. "I think it's some of my best work."

"You're no Langston Hughes, so don't quit your day job!"

Hanging his head, he sniffed and pretended to wipe a tear away from his eyes.

Karma giggled. She couldn't believe this was the same guy who'd barged into her shop a week ago and caused a scene. At brunch, one of the guests had asked how long they'd been dating, and before Karma could answer, Morrison had surprised her with a kiss. Then he'd told the group about meeting her at her salon, and apologized again for his behavior.

Karma tossed aside the white tissue paper, and gasped, glancing from the gift bag to Morrison, and back again. Inside was an alligator-skin Hermès wallet, the most coveted accessory of the season. She'd been saving up for months to buy one and wondered if Reagan had told her uncle about Karma's obsession with designer purses. She wanted to cheer, but since she wasn't going to keep the shiny, orange wallet, she tempered her excitement. "When did you get this? Who told you I've been saving up to buy one?"

"A man of mystery never shares his secrets. Do you like it?"

"Yes, of course, but it's too expensive. It costs thousands of dollars, and—"

"Karma, it's a birthday gift. No strings attached," he said, interrupting her.

Staring longingly at the wallet, she drew her fingertips across the shiny, silver buckle. Morrison came from money, but Karma still felt uncomfortable accepting the ridiculously expensive birthday gift. Days earlier at the salon, she'd overheard two divorcées discussing the Drake family and listened closely. Morrison had two younger brothers, and after the death of his sister, Emmanuelle, he'd become Reagan's legal guardian. The Drake family had been on the Hamptons power list for decades, and although Morrison's father, Nathaniel, had been an esteemed Supreme Court judge, it was his mother, Viola, who'd put the family on the map. The talented interior designer, who her well-heeled clients affectionately nicknamed L'élu, which meant "The Chosen One" in French, had retired a multimillionaire. Morrison was filthy rich, but Karma couldn't accept the gift. She didn't want him to think she was swayed by money. She wasn't. She had as much fun at the bowling alley as she did at A-list parties, and it didn't matter how long Karma lived in the Hamptons, she'd never forget her humble roots.

"I can't accept it," she said, shaking her head. "It's too much. It wouldn't be right."

"Okay, I understand. Let's not argue about it. I hate going to the mall to return things, so I'll just give it to Reagan. Problem solved."

Morrison reached for the gift bag, and Karma slapped his hand away.

"You can't give this beautiful wallet to Reagan. She won't take good care of it."

"I know. She'll probably lose it, or accidently spill her latte on it—"

"I changed my mind. I'll keep it. Thanks, Morrison. I love it," she confessed, a smile overwhelming her mouth. "You shouldn't have, but am I ever glad you did!"

Chuckling, he took the champagne bottle out of the ice bucket. Morrison opened it, filled two glasses and handed her one. "A toast to the birthday girl," he said, raising his flute in the air. "May this be the best year of your life, and may all your hopes and dreams come true."

They clinked glasses, then tasted their drinks.

"Morrison, I can't believe you went to all this trouble for me."

"It's no trouble at all. It's your thirtieth birthday. You have to celebrate big."

"Where are we going?" Karma wanted to grab her cell phone from her purse, so she could blog about her new designer wallet, but since she didn't want Morrison to think she was rude, Karma kept her hands on her lap and off her clutch purse.

"We don't have to be at the theater until seven o'clock," he said, glancing at his wristwatch. "We have several hours to explore the city, so I figured we'd check out the botanical garden."

"I love the botanical garden, and was planning to go there next week to see their latest exhibits. Hey, have you been snooping through my social media pages?"

"Me? Snoop?" He affected a French accent. "I'm a judge, *mon chérie*, not a spy."

Fond memories filled her mind. "When I was a kid, my mom used to take me to the botanical garden almost every Sunday. We'd walk the grounds, have a picnic and chocolate ice cream. I always enjoyed spending the day there, but it's been years since I visited."

"Me too. I used to take Reagan all the time, but now she's too cool to be seen with me in public. Go figure. Just because I'm a judge doesn't mean I'm old and uptight."

"Damn right you're not," Karma said. "You're a youthful, charismatic man, with impeccable style, who can have any woman you want."

"Is that right? Does that mean I can have you? Right here, right now?"

His eyes bore into her, but she could tell by the amused expression on his face that he was joking. Karma wasn't.

Accepting his challenge, she kicked off her sandals and climbed onto his lap. Thankful the privacy barrier was raised, and the driver couldn't see them, Karma draped her arms around his neck and rocked her hips slowly back and forth. His erection came to life, poking her inner thigh, giving her a rush.

"Karma, what are you doing?" Morrison asked, wetting his lips with his tongue.

"Showing my appreciation for my incredible birthday gift."

"But we're only a few minutes away from the botanical garden."

A smirk curled her lips. "Then, you better cum quickly."

Nothing could wipe the smile off Karma's face. Exiting the iconic Harlem theater on Morrison's arm, they joined the slow-moving crowd meandering along Malcolm X Boulevard, chatting and laughing about the play. Karma snuggled against his shoulder. All afternoon, Morrison had been attentive and affectionate, and it was hard not to fantasize about him being her boyfriend. He treated her as if she was special to him, and for as long as Karma lived she'd never forget their romantic marathon date in the city.

Karma reflected on their day together. Their first stop had been to the botanical garden, and the tranquil setting was a breathtaking oasis, filled with vibrant colors and tropical fragrances. Instead of taking the tram through the fifty-two-acre garden, they'd walked hand in hand. They'd enjoyed reading the signs of the trees, flowers and exotic plants. The groundskeepers were knowledgeable and friendly, the conservatory offered classes on horticulture, and the rolling hills, towering trees and ornamental

conifers looked like something out of a Dr. Seuss book.
Beauty was in every inch of the garden, and the artwork
displayed by renowned artists were striking. Happy to
escape the hustle and bustle of the city for a few hours,
Karma had sat down on a wooden bench and soaked in
the serene atmosphere.

The botanical garden was as magical as Karma remembered, and as she'd gazed at the water lilies thoughts
of her mother filled her mind. It was hard to believe
she'd been gone for six years. Seemed like just yesterday
they were going for mother-daughter mani-pedis, and
whipping up decadent desserts in their small, cramped
kitchen, singing along with the radio.

"Are you having a good birthday?"

Surfacing from her thoughts, Karma focused on the
here and now. "You don't even have to ask. This is the
best birthday I've ever had, and I will remember it for-
evahhh."

Morrison chuckled, and the sound of his hearty laugh
made Karma smile.

"What did you enjoy the most? The botanical garden,
the museum or the play?"

Cocking her head to the right, she took a moment to
consider the question. Karma remembered the outrageous
signs inside the Museum of Sex—warning people not to
lick, stroke or mount the exhibits—and laughed to herself. They'd stopped at the museum on the way to the theater and spent an hour perusing the evocative displays. In
the apparel store, Morrison had bought her hundreds of
dollars' worth of merchandise, and Karma was anxious
to try out the sex toys, wanted to end the evening making love to him. It was the longest date Karma had ever
been on, but she wasn't ready to call it a night. During
the play's intermission, Morrison had suggested having

drinks at a local cocktail lounge, and even though Karma had to be at the salon bright and early in the morning, she wanted to check out the popular Harlem bar.

"They were all incredible, and I couldn't have asked for a better birthday, but if I had to choose one I'd pick the play. *Husband for Hire* was hilarious! The music was outstanding, the acting was top-notch and I laughed until I cried during the funeral scene!"

"I bet you worked up quite an appetite during the play," Morrison said, gazing down at her. "You must be starving. Do you want to eat at one of the nearby soul food restaurants?"

"No, actually, I'm still full from dinner, but I'd love a cocktail."

"Then we'll go to the Cove. They make the best martinis in the city."

Spotting the limo across the street, Karma said, "Let's walk. It's a beautiful night, and we've eaten so much junk food today we could use the exercise."

"Speak for yourself. I'm in tip-top shape," Morrison bragged, flexing his arm muscles.

That you are, Karma thought, remembering how he'd picked her up and carried her into the master bedroom last night. *Just thinking about your rock-hard body is making me wet!*

"Are you sure you don't want to use the limo? The lounge is several miles from here."

Unable to resist teasing him, Karma poked a finger at his broad chest. "What's wrong, Mr. Tip-Top Shape? Don't think you can hang?"

"Oh, I can hang," he said with a twinkle in his eye. "*You* of all people should know that. You had no complaints in the bedroom, and if my memory serves me correctly *you're* the one who requested a break after our quickie, not me."

His words, and the devilish grin on his face, caused goose bumps to ripple across her skin. No one had ever gone all out for her birthday, or fulfilled her every desire in the bedroom. Karma knew it was impossible to fall in love with someone in twenty-four hours, but her feelings for Morrison were so strong they scared her.

"Is the Hamptons home for you? Are you planning to be there long-term?"

Karma took a moment to consider his question. "I don't know. My dream is to open salons all across the country, so there's no telling where I'll end up. What about you? Would you like to settle down and raise a family in your hometown?"

"That depends on whether or not you're applying for the position of Mrs. Morrison Drake," he teased, squeezing her arm. "I like the sound of Karma Drake, don't you?"

He laughed, and Karma did too, though for some reason the thought of being his wife excited her, caused her heart to dance inside her chest. They joked around with each other, talked nonstop, and Karma could open up to him in ways she couldn't with past boyfriends. This was only their first date, but she was ready to delete her online dating profiles.

"The Hamptons will always be home," Morrison continued. "But if I'm appointed to the Supreme Court in the near future I'll have to relocate to Washington, and I'm okay with that."

"The Supreme Court, huh? You have some pretty lofty goals," she said, raising her eyebrows for effect. "Is there a lot of competition? What is the process like?"

"Long, arduous and stressful, but I'm determined to

achieve my goal, and nothing is going to stop me from being appointed to the highest court in the nation."

"I don't know much about the Supreme Court," Karma confessed with a sheepish smile. "I'm more of a Food Network girl than a CNN girl, and to be honest politics bore me."

"I'm obsessed with the news, and I can't go to bed without watching my boy Wolf Blitzer," Morrison joked. "The first time I saw my dad in his robe, I knew I wanted to follow in his footsteps, and in law school I gained a deep respect for the justice system. It fascinates me, and every day I learn something new…"

Strolling through Harlem, soaking up the energy and ambience of the community, they peered inside shop windows, perused an African American art gallery hosting a poetry reading and stopped at the intersection to watch a group of female break-dancers. Karma remembered the last time she'd been to the area with Jazz, and sighed inwardly. Jazz had texted her that morning with a birthday message, but Karma hadn't responded yet. Was still hurt that her best friend had ditched her for a guy. She was having fun with Morrison, and would never forget their romantic night at her favorite luxury hotel, but she was disappointed in Jazz.

Stylish and sophisticated, with outdoor seating, sultry lights and soft music, Cove Lounge catered to an over-thirty crowd. Finding a table inside, they placed their drink order with the middle-aged waiter, and perused the one-page menu. "This place reminds me of The Palm East Hampton," she said, admiring the tasteful decor. "Every Monday night, I attend Networking After Dark at the restaurant bar, and end up meeting locals, chatting with other professionals and eating more than a woman pregnant with twins. I love it, but my waistline doesn't!"

Morrison raised an eyebrow. "Networking After Dark? Never heard of it."

"You need to get out more. All work and no play makes Morrison a dull boy," Karma teased, in a sing-song voice. "Networking After Dark is an opportunity for small business owners and professionals to connect, and the relationships I've formed over the past year have led to increased profits for Beauty by Karma and more recognition in the community."

Her cell phone lit up, and she glanced at the screen. Not wanting any distractions, she'd put her cell on silent that morning, but Karma couldn't resist checking it from time to time, and smiled when she saw her newest social media notification. Picking up her cell, she showed it to Morrison. "Your niece should be a model. She looks incredible in this picture."

Peering at the screen, Morrison gripped the iPhone in his hands. "She got a tattoo! I never gave her permission to get one. Is she out of her mind? What was she thinking?"

Surprised by his outburst, Karma pried her cell from his hands, and leaned back in her chair. Curious to see why Morrison was upset, she scrutinized the picture Reagan had posted on her social media page. "She has a tiny, floral design on the inside of her wrist that you have to squint to see. I think it's simple, feminine and cute."

"And I think it's stupid."

"Morrison, relax, Reagan's a good girl. You have nothing to worry about."

A waitress arrived with their drinks, and Karma tasted her watermelon martini. It was strong, but sweet, just the way she liked it. Sipping her drink, she noticed Morrison's stiff posture and touched his hand. It was cold, like the expression on his face, but Karma knew what to say to turn his frown into a smile.

"When Reagan came by the salon on Friday afternoon, she mentioned there's a good chance she'll be named valedictorian of her graduating class. You must be so proud of her."

"What was she doing at the salon?" he asked, leaning forward in his chair, his eyes so dark they looked black, not brown. "Reagan was supposed to be with her study group."

"She stopped by to show me her grad pictures. Is that a problem?"

Annoyed, Karma struggled to control her temper.

"You don't have children, so you have no idea what it's like to be a parent."

"That's the problem. Reagan isn't a child anymore. She's an intelligent young woman, with her own thoughts and opinions, and the more you try to control her the more she'll rebel."

"In my experience, kids need a firm, hard hand or they'll run wild," he said, in a stern, authoritative voice. "I don't want my niece to lose sight of her goals, and no offense, Karma, but they don't involve doing hair and makeup for the rest of her life."

Offended by his remarks, Karma stared him down. "You're right, I don't have children, but I've been around kids my whole life, and—"

"In what capacity? Babysitting for a few hours a week?"

"No, I've been a mentor for the Boys and Girls Club for over a decade."

"Volunteering is admirable, but it doesn't compare with parenting on a daily basis. I've been Reagan's legal guardian since she was seven years old, and she means the world to me."

His expression softened, and sadness flickered in his eyes.

"What was your sister like?" Karma asked, moved by his words about his niece. An only child, she'd always envied people with siblings, and wished she had brothers and sisters to love.

"Emmanuelle was mischievous, strong-willed and passionate about life, and I want to honor her memory by ensuring Reagan fulfills her dreams of becoming a human rights attorney. I appreciate your concern, Karma, but I know what's best for Reagan, not you."

"I never said I did. I'm simply giving you some friendly advice."

"I don't need it," he snapped. "I know what I'm doing."

"If you knew what you were doing, Reagan wouldn't feel the need to lie to you."

Karma didn't realize the thought had escaped her mouth until Morrison scoffed.

"You don't understand."

"No, *you* don't understand," she snapped back, determined to speak her mind. He was a good man who'd stepped up to take care of his niece after his sister's death, but that didn't mean Morrison was right about everything—he wasn't.

Karma exhaled. Had she made a mistake hooking up with him? Morrison was an outstanding lover, with exquisite skills in the bedroom, but he was the most stubborn, hardheaded man she'd ever met, and his superior, know-it-all attitude grated on her nerves. "You have to give Reagan the room to grow, to learn from her mistakes, or she'll never become a strong, independent woman capable of standing on her own two feet."

"I disagree, and since we're discussing my niece, I want you to revise her schedule. Reagan can work two four-hour shifts a week, and that's it. If it were up to me she wouldn't be working at your salon at all, but I'm willing to compromise."

"Have you talked to Reagan about this?"

"Yes, but she won't listen to me. That's why I'm speaking to you privately."

Karma shook her head. "No. I won't do that to her. She's an incredible talent, and if I cut her hours she'll be upset, and I don't want to hurt her feelings."

"I thought we were having a good time together. I thought we were friends."

"We are, but Reagan's important to me, and I won't betray her trust."

"You have to fire her, then. If you don't, it could jeopardize her future."

A lightbulb went off in her head. "Is that why you offered to spend my birthday with me? Because you thought you could convince me to do what you want?"

"I'm here because you're a vivacious, captivating woman."

"No," she argued, mad at herself for falling for his good-guy act at the wedding reception. "You're here because you think you can use sex to control me."

"If that was true we'd still be in my suite making love. You were the one who wanted to go out, not me. I was perfectly content holding you in my arms."

Silence fell across their cozy, corner table. The waiter returned, and to Karma's surprise Morrison asked for the check. Their argument had put a damper on her good mood, made her rethink inviting him back to her place when they returned to the Hamptons at the end of the night. He wouldn't look at her, didn't speak.

Not wanting to end the date on a sour note, she said, "Morrison, I can't thank you enough for today. I've had a lot of great birthdays, but this ranks as the all-time best, and I'm deeply grateful."

"You're welcome. It was my pleasure," he replied with a curt nod, but his body language said, "Whatever." Morrison was mad at her, angry because she'd disagreed with him, and it was a turnoff. His narrow-mindedness annoyed her, and even though they were in perfect sync in the bedroom, it was obvious they'd never make it as a couple.

Exiting the lounge minutes later, Karma sensed Morrison's frustration, and decided this would be their first and last date. They'd had a remarkable night together, but that's all it was—one magical night. And, if she'd learned anything from the death of her mother, it was to know when to walk away, and that's exactly what Karma was going to do: forget Morrison, and move on.

Chapter 9

"You Honor… Your Honor…are you okay?" Vicente Torres asked in a hushed tone of voice.

Morrison blinked, realized everyone inside Courtroom 6 at the East Hampton Justice Court was staring at him, and wondered how long he'd been sitting behind his desk, fantasizing about Karma. Reliving their explosive night together in his Four Seasons hotel suite three days earlier. They hadn't spoken since he'd dropped her off at her condominium on Sunday night. Their goodbyes had been awkward, as if they were strangers who didn't like each other, but they did. They'd hit it off during their date, made an instant connection. She'd opened up to him about her family, her career goals, the teenage girls she mentored and even her past relationships. He'd done the same. And, even though they'd argued at Cove Lounge, Morrison still desired her. Wanted to see her. Longed to talk to her, to kiss her, to make love—

"Your Honor, you have one more case on the docket before lunch. Do you think you can handle it, or should we adjourn for the day?"

Morrison broke free of his thoughts. He had to get

his head in the game. Couldn't risk daydreaming again. His silver-haired bailiff, Vicente, was standing to his left with a concerned expression on his slim face, and Morrison nodded to let the ex-cop know everything was kosher. Morrison didn't know what had gotten into him. He couldn't believe he'd lost his focus in court. Law was his passion, what excited him, and he prided himself on being professional at all times. Sure, he'd had some drinks with dinner last night, but it wasn't enough to get him drunk. He felt out of it, like an addict desperate for his next fix, and Karma was his drug. His weakness. The only woman he wanted. Craved. Needed in his bed.

To regain control, Morrison drank the ice-cold water in his glass. It had been a busy morning. For the past three hours, he'd been presiding over cases concerning legal disputes and traffic offenses, but at noon he'd break for lunch and enjoy some downtime in his chambers. In the afternoon, he'd read documents on pleadings and motions, research legal issues, write judgments and review upcoming cases.

Straightening in his chair, Morrison called the next name on the alphabetized list.

"I'm Mrs. Syà Nguyen," a woman said, rising to her feet and exiting the gallery.

Contrary to what tourists thought, everyone in the Hamptons wasn't a millionaire, and it was obvious the woman of Asian descent, with the stringy brown hair, shuffling down the aisle, was lower income. Her head was bent, and she was twisting the gold, wedding band on her left hand. "How do you plea, Mrs. Nguyen?"

"Guilty...not guilty...oh, I don't know."

Confused by her plea, Morrison consulted the documents in front of him. "You were clocked going sixty miles per hour on Montauk Highway on February 3.

That's twenty-five miles over the speed limit. Why were you speeding?"

"I wasn't paying attention... I was upset... I wasn't thinking clearly..."

Her voice was so low Morrison had to strain to hear her. "Why were you upset?"

"I'd gone shopping for the first time since having my twin boys, and...and...and..." Sniffing, she wiped her cheeks with the back of her hands. "Nothing fit right. Everything I tried on was tight and uncomfortable, and I left the mall empty-handed."

Sympathizing with the young mother, Morrison nodded in understanding. His mind transported him back to the afternoon he'd gone shopping with Emmanuelle and one-year-old Reagan. An hour after arriving at the Chanel boutique, his sister had burst into tears and fled the store. Catching up to her in the parking lot, he'd learned that none of the dresses Emmanuelle liked fit her new, voluptuous, post-baby shape. To cheer her up, he'd treated her to ice cream, and promised to help her lose the baby weight. And, they did, one Zumba class at a time. "I'll reduce your ticket to fifty dollars, but I don't want to see you in my court again, Ms. Nguyen," he said, in a stern voice. "Speeding is the leading cause of all traffic accidents, and your twins need their mother, so please be more careful out on the roads."

Her face lit up. Clasping her hands, she bowed her head in gratitude. "Thank you, Your Honor. Thank you so very much."

Embarrassed by her effusive praise, Morrison struck his gavel against the desk to call for silence and to signal the end of the day's session. "Court adjourned."

Entering his chambers seconds later, Morrison took off his robe, hung it in the closet and dropped into one of the leather armchairs in front of his desk. He took his cell out of the drawer and checked for missed calls and texts. He didn't have any.

Sunshine filled the office. It was warm and sunny outside, the perfect weather for swimming or having a picnic, and as he gazed at the windows Morrison wished he was at the beach with Karma.

His thoughts returned to Sunday night, and Morrison winced. One minute they were flirting and laughing at their table; the next minute they were bickering and fighting like an old married couple. He owed Karma an apology, but he couldn't bring himself to call her. Couldn't make his mouth form the words. His father had taught him that *real men don't apologize*, and Morrison didn't know if he could swallow his pride, and admit that he was wrong. He shouldn't have insulted her or raised his voice and knew it would take a huge gesture to make up for what he'd done. That's why he'd sent several edible arrangements to Beauty by Karma that morning. He'd expected to hear from Karma hours ago, but still no phone call.

Morrison rubbed his neck, trying to relieve the soreness in his muscles. He was starving, but he didn't want to eat until he spoke to Karma. Had to make things right with her, before the chasm between them grew and he lost the opportunity to take her out on a second date.

Wanting to hear her voice, Morrison punched in his password, then dialed Karma's cell phone number. He was sweating like an ax murderer on the witness stand, but he blew out a deep breath and put his cell to his ear, hoping he hadn't blown his chance with the most vivacious woman he had ever met.

Karma spotted an empty space directly in front of Beauty by Karma and cheered. *This day just keeps get-*

ting better! she thought, punching the gas pedal with her peep-toe sandals. Flicking on her right-turn signal, she switched lanes and parked her pink PT Cruiser behind the luxury SUV with the out-of-state license plates. Karma closed the sunroof, grabbed her things from the passenger seat and activated the alarm.

Carrying her bags and boxes of gourmet cookies in her arms, Karma heard her cell phone ringing inside her purse and decided to let the call go to voice mail. It was probably a client wanting to make an appointment, but Karma needed a moment to catch her breath. All morning, she'd been running from one appointment to the next, and if she wanted to have the energy to work in the afternoon she had to eat something of sustenance, and junk food wasn't it. Once she dropped off the treats for her staff, and checked in with Jazz, she'd suggest they have lunch at the vegan restaurant across the street. Things had been strained between them ever since Karma's birthday, but she was ready to put the past behind them and move on. She wanted the expansion project to go smoothly, and needed Jazz's support and keen business sense to make it happen. They were a dynamic duo who were destined for greatness in the stylist world, and Karma wasn't going to let anything come between them.

"You look like you could use a hand. Let me help you," said a male voice.

Before Karma could protest, the man in the striped dress shirt and navy pants took the boxes from her hands and followed her into the salon. The waiting area was empty, but every chair in the salon was filled. The air held a tantalizing scent, pop music was playing on the stereo system, and the atmosphere was loud and lively.

"Great, you're here!" the colorist said with a sigh of relief. "Do you mind covering the front desk? Abigail's on lunch, and I have to clean the sinks before my next client arrives."

"No problem, Eve. I'll hold down the fort until Abigail gets back, but take the cookies into the salon and make sure all of the customers have one."

Marching around the front desk, the colorist took the boxes from the stranger's outstretched hands and traipsed off, shaking her broad hips to the beat of the music.

"Thank you for your help. That was very kind of you," Karma said with a polite smile.

"It was my pleasure. I'm Tiago Van den Berg of Van den Berg Realty and you are?"

"Karma Sullivan. Welcome to my salon, Beauty by Karma."

"Impressive." Nodding, he slid his hands in his pockets and slowly glanced around the shop. "I've been looking for a new barber. Maybe I should book an appointment."

"Sounds good. I'll get one of our talented male stylists to come speak to you."

Eager to get to her office to touch base with Jazz, Karma waved goodbye and spun around.

The stranger touched her arm, stopping her in her tracks. "Can I have your number?" he asked. "I'd love to take you out sometime."

Average height, with tanned skin and a slim build, Karma guessed Tiago was in his forties, and checked his left hand for a wedding ring. He wasn't wearing one, but she paused to consider his request. Normally, Karma didn't give her cell number to strange men, but the Van den Berg family were real estate giants, and she wanted to pick his brain about the housing market. The lease on her East Hampton condo was up at the end of the year, and Karma was ready to buy her first home. Furthermore, the more successful, influential people she knew in the

Hamptons the better. Karma plucked a pink business card out of one of the decorative card holders on the counter and handed it to him. "Here's my card."

"Awesome. I'll call you tonight."

"I look forward to hearing from you, Tiago, and thanks again for your help."

Watching him exit the salon, Karma had second thoughts about giving him her number. He was attractive, in a scholarly way, but he didn't light her fire. Didn't excite her. Not the way Morrison did. Karma caught herself, told herself to stop thinking about him. It didn't work. Remembering the things they'd done in his suite made her pulse thunder in her ears. *What's the matter with me? Why am I fantasizing about Morrison? Why can't I get him out of my mind?*

"Look at you!" shrieked the nail technician, sashaying into the waiting area with a hand stuck to her hip. "First, a romantic night in the city with Morrison Drake, and now a date with that blue-eyed, pretty boy, Tiago Van den Berg. Guuurrrl, this is your week!"

Karma ignored the comment, knew if she responded the nail technician, Poppy Castelo, would grill her about her night with Morrison, and she didn't want to talk about it. She'd planned to keep it a secret, but one of the couples they'd had brunch with at the Four Seasons Hotel had blabbed to one of the stylists, and now everyone knew she'd spent the weekend with Morrison. "Where's Jazz?" she asked, sliding behind the counter to double-check the afternoon schedule.

"No idea. She hasn't been in all day, but I overheard one of the stylists say she's sick."

Again! But she called in sick yesterday. Karma wasn't buying it; didn't believe for a second her best friend was ill. She knew from checking Jazz's social media pages that her bestie had tickets to the Shakira concert that evening, and Karma would bet every dollar in her bank account that Jazz was living it up in the city. She didn't get it. Didn't understand why her best friend was screwing her over. Flaking on their clients and staff.

Looking through the mail, one of the envelopes stuck out from the pile. It was handwritten, but Karma didn't recognize the penmanship. She ripped it open and scanned the paper. Her eyes widened. *This can't be real. This can't be happening. How did Feisal find me!*

Panic seized her heart, and the paper fell from her hands. The room swam around her, but Karma picked up the letter, ripped it to pieces and dropped it in the garbage bin under the reception desk.

Karma took a moment to gather herself. To collect her thoughts. She hadn't seen or heard from Feisal in years, and wondered how he'd found her. Had her grandparents told him? Had they given him her address? No, that was impossible. They hated Feisal more than she did, and would never give him her contact information. It didn't matter. He was in jail, where he belonged, and she wasn't responding to his letter. Not today, not ever—

"Can I have some of this? I'm starving, and I *love* exotic fruit."

Snapping out of her thoughts, Karma followed Poppy's gaze. Noticing, for the first time, the colorful fruit baskets sitting on the glass coffee table, she smiled. There were cupcake-shaped pineapples, chocolate-dipped mango, heart-shaped papaya, guava covered in sprinkles, and marshmallows. "They're so cute! Who sent them?"

"Beats me," she said, popping a caramel-coated strawberry into her mouth. "I wasn't here when they were delivered, but there should be a card around here somewhere."

Fear consumed her, made Karma quiver and sweat. Were the edible arrangements from Feisal? Had he ordered them from prison? If he did, she was dumping them in the trash. As she spotted the note taped to the side of the yellow basket dread filled her stomach.

"I'll be right back." Poppy picked up a basket and left.

Glad she was alone in the reception area, Karma read the short, typed message, hoping against all hope it wasn't from Feisal—a man she despised.

To the sexiest woman in the Hamptons. You're more beautiful than any flower, and I hope the fruit bouquet satisfies your sweet tooth until our next date.
From, Morrison,
Your birthday bae

Laughing out loud, Karma dropped the note inside her purse and retrieved her cell phone. She had dozens of text messages from customers, but she decided to return Morrison's call first. Wanted to thank him for the generous, unexpected gift. Karma considered going to her office so she could have some privacy, but remembered Jazz was a no-show and she had to cover the front desk while Abigail was taking her lunch break.

"The chocolate-dipped mango is addictive, and totally worth the calories!" Poppy said with a laugh. Returning to the waiting area, she picked up two more bouquets and returned to the salon floor. Happy her clients and staff were eating the edible arrangements, Karma flashed a thumbs-up at Poppy.

Morrison answered his cell phone on the first ring, and the sound of his deep, masculine voice made her skin tingle. "Hi, Morrison. It's me, Karma," she said, wishing she didn't sound nervous and breathless. "I'm calling to thank you for the fruit bouquets. They're beautiful, and delicious, and everyone in the salon is enjoying them."

"You're welcome. It's a peace offering and—"

"A peace offering?" Karma repeated, wrinkling her nose. "Are we at war?"

"We argued on Sunday and I didn't want there to be any hard feelings between us. I had a great time with you last weekend, and I want to see you again."

Karma hardened her heart. Had to. Safeguarding her feelings against Morrison was paramount. Not because she was scared of him hurting her, but because she was scared of hurting him. There were things about her he didn't know, things she'd never confided in anyone, not even her closest friends, and she could never tell Morrison the truth about her past. It was too painful, and Karma didn't want anyone to know her shameful family secret.

"Morrison, I'm fine. Like you said, I don't have any children and should mind my own business, and from now on that's what I'm going to do. You don't have to worry about me giving Reagan advice or cramming my opinions down your throat, either."

"Karma, I never said that."

"You didn't have to. You made it perfectly clear that you don't need or want my help with Reagan." He couldn't see her, but she fervently shook her head. "And I have to respect your feelings. You're her legal guardian, and you know what's best for her, not me."

"Let's talk tonight over dinner. What time should I pick you up?"

"Sorry, Morrison. I have to work."

"But the salon closes at eight o'clock. That's plenty of time for us to grab a bite to eat."

"My celebrity clients prefer having their hair and

makeup done in the comfort of their own home, rather than coming down to the salon, so after I close up the shop, I do home consultations until ten or eleven o'clock."

He whistled. "I thought I worked long hours, but I'm a slacker compared to you!"

Karma laughed at his joke. "I've been working eighty hours a week for years, but I have no complaints. I love my life, my salon and my clients, and I'll do anything to succeed."

"Do you still want to see the new *Oceans* movie? Last weekend, you mentioned being a huge fan of the franchise, and I have tickets for the advance screening on Saturday," he said. "The movie doesn't start until ten, so we can have dinner at Arbor Restaurant first…"

Staring down at her cell phone, Karma wondered if she'd heard him correctly. The salon was loud, but his strong voice cut through the noise. No, she wasn't hearing things. He'd asked her out again—the second time in minutes.

Tasting a piece of guava, Karma chewed slowly. It was sweet, just like the man who'd sent them. She was careful with her words, didn't want to say anything to offend him, especially after everything he'd done to make her birthday special, but Karma had to speak the truth. "Morrison, I like you, and I think you're a great guy, but I don't think we should date. We had our fun at the Four Seasons, but that's all it was. One, incredible weekend."

"What if I want more?"

Then, you should find a quiet, docile woman to date, because that's not me! Out of her peripheral vision, she noticed Abigail headed toward her, and knew it was time to end the call. "Morrison, I have to go, but thanks again for the fruit bouquets."

Karma pressed the end button, grabbed her bags off

the floor and made a beeline for her office before her gossip-hungry receptionist questioned her about the edible arrangements. If her staff knew Morrison had sent them, they'd hound her relentlessly.

Karma threw open the office door. With a heavy heart, she sat down behind her office desk, kicked off her shoes and touched the Picture app on her cell phone. Photos from her birthday—at the botanical garden with Morrison, posing in front of the Museum of Sex, smiling in her cushy theater seat, dancing in the limousine—filled the screen. Thoughts of Morrison came to mind, but she pushed them aside, refused to think about the handsome, intelligent man she'd spent the weekend with. He wasn't happy unless he was calling the shots, and although he'd rocked her world between the sheets she'd rather be alone than with someone who didn't respect her opinion.

If that's true, her inner voice challenged, *then why do you regret turning down his dinner invitation? Why do you wish he was here with you now?*

Stumped, Karma realized she didn't have an answer, or any hope of ever forgetting Morrison, and her sadness was so profound her heart throbbed in pain.

Chapter 10

"Guys, sorry I'm late." Roderick's footsteps and his loud, booming voice cut through the eerie silence at the Westlake Marina on Sunday morning. "Toya got back late from her spin class, and I didn't want to leave until I spoke to her about my plans for the day."

Duane and Morrison exchanged a look, then shook their heads in disbelief.

"That's why you're an hour late for our fishing trip? Because you had to get permission from your fiancée to spend the day with us? Roderick, are you effing kidding me?"

"It's not like that. We got into another argument about the wedding last night, and I wanted to make sure we were cool before I left to go fishing," he explained, shrugging a shoulder. "Duane, you're married. You know how it is."

"No, I don't. Erikah and I have a great relationship, and I don't need her permission to go fishing with you guys, or anything else for that matter. She's my wife, not my parole officer."

Morrison gripped the wheel of the boat, and steered

it away from the dock. Sunrise was the best time to fish, but because of Roderick they were an hour behind schedule. They'd be lucky if they caught anything for lunch, but Morrison kept his thoughts to himself, didn't want to make his brother feel worse than he already did. He looked remorseful, but Morrison wasn't ready to let him off the hook. "You should have called. We were worried about you."

Roderick scoffed. "Mo, relax, I'm fine. You worry too much…"

Tuning his brother out, Morrison took in his surroundings. The air was thick, and the sky was hazy, but it didn't detract from the beauty around him. Home to some of the most beautiful views and sunsets in the country, the Hamptons was one of the prettiest places Morrison had ever seen, and he loved living there. Though, when he was appointed to the Supreme Court he'd gladly pack his bags and relocate to Washington.

"Mo, slow down," Roderick said, gesturing to the water with a flap of his hand. "This is the perfect spot. This is where I caught that ten-pound trout last summer."

"Yeah, in your dreams." Duane clapped him hard on the shoulder. "Dad caught it, and you helped him haul it into the boat. That's it."

Roderick raised an eyebrow. "Is that what happened?"

Morrison and Duane nodded, and Roderick wore a sheepish smile.

"I drank a lot of whiskey that night, and to be honest the details are sketchy in my mind."

Tell us something we don't know. Morrison couldn't believe how much his brother had changed in the last six months. Roderick used to be active and fit, but his partying lifestyle had finally caught up to him, and now he had round cheeks, a beer belly and flabby arms. He was a functional alcoholic who refused to believe he had a problem, and Morrison feared it was just a matter of time before he lost his prestigious job at the best entertainment law firm in Manhattan.

"Mo, let's test the waters." Duane rubbed his hands together. "I'm feeling lucky."

"You sound like Dad," Roderick joked. "Too bad you can't fish like him!"

As the clouds parted, the sun emerged and the mansions dotting the shore faded into the background. Gazing at the crystal-clear water, Morrison remembered all the times their dad had taken them fishing when they were kids, and wore a sad smile. They'd spend hours at the lake, cracking jokes, playing Frisbee, goofing around, and he'd never forget how much fun they'd had together. Morrison wished his father was healthy enough to join them on their monthly boating trips, but made a mental note to take a video of their outing to send to his dad. In the afternoon, they'd return to their family estate, barbecue their fresh catch and have lunch with their parents.

Morrison turned off the boat. He grabbed his fishing rod, put a piece of bacon on the hook and cast his line into the deep. Staring intently at the water, looking for movement, he searched for signs of life down below. Helicopters flew overhead, ferrying the rich and famous to and from the city and disrupting the tranquil scenery, but Morrison saw fish swimming beneath the surface, and hoped he caught some striped sea bass for lunch.

Birds chirped, the breeze whistled through the trees around the lake, and the sun climbed high in the brilliant, blue sky. It was the perfect escape from his demanding, nonstop schedule, and there was nowhere else in the world Morrison would rather be.

Except with Karma, said his inner voice. *She won't see you, and you're frustrated.*

Damn right, I'm frustrated, Morrison thought, gripping his fishing rod. He'd sent her a peace offering and apologized for his behavior at the lounge, but she was still giving him the cold shoulder, and he was sick of it. All week, he'd called her with no success. And, when he'd asked Reagan about her shift at the salon yesterday, and she'd casually mentioned that Karma had left in the afternoon with a Channing Tatum look-alike, his shoulders sank. Was that why Karma wasn't returning his calls and texts? Because she was dating someone else? For the first time in his life, Morrison wished he was on social media. Wished he could see what she was up to, who she was spending her time with—

"Hey, were you at the Cove Lounge last Sunday night? Toya was there with a friend, and she thought she caught a glimpse of you, but she didn't recognize the woman you were with."

"I was with Karma Sullivan, the owner of the beauty salon Reagan works at."

"Don't know her. Is she hot?"

Morrison grinned. "Do you like partying with Rihanna?"

"Hell yeah! RiRi is mad cool, not to mention fine as hell."

"And so is Karma. She's smart and vivacious, and I enjoy her company."

Duane grinned. "Nothing like a hot summer fling to get the juices going."

Morrison kept his thoughts to himself, didn't reveal his true feelings to his brothers, but he wanted more than a fling with Karma, liked the idea of them being exclusive. Her fiery personality left him wanting more, and these days the salon owner was all he could think about. *How am I supposed to sweep Karma off her feet when she won't give me the time of day? What will it take to get back in her good books?*

"I'm starving," Roderick announced, patting his stomach. "Where's the food?"

"Keep your voice down. You'll scare the fish."

"Damn, D, we're in a boat, not the library. If you wanted peace and quiet you should have stayed home!" Roderick gave a hearty laugh, then jabbed his brothers in the sides with his elbows. "Now point me in the direction of the cooler, so I can have breakfast."

Roderick propped his fishing rod up against the bench and marched to the back of the boat, whistling with gusto. "There's only fruit, sandwiches and bottled water in here," he complained taking off his aviator-style sunglasses. "Where's the booze?"

Morrison was annoyed, but he spoke in a calm voice. "I didn't bring any—"

"Why not? Who goes fishing without beer? Drinking is what makes the trip fun."

"You always overdo it, and I didn't want to risk you getting sick again."

"This is whack." Roderick slammed the cooler shut. "I don't need this shit. Turn the boat around. I'm going home."

Duane narrowed his gaze. "Did you come here to drink, or to hang out with us?"

"Both. I'm stressed, and I need something to help me relax." Hanging his head, he threw his hands in the air and paced the length of the boat. "You shouldn't be ganging up on me. I'm going through hell at home, and at work and…it's…it's too much."

At first glance, Morrison thought Roderick was crying. His behavior was telling, and since nothing mattered more to him than his family, he set aside his fishing rod and approached Roderick. "What's going on, bro? What's wrong?"

"Everything. I screwed up, and it could cost me my career, my reputation and my relationship."

Joining them at the rear of the boat, Duane said, "Bro, we can't help you fix things if you don't tell us what's wrong."

"Last year, one of the new attorneys suggested I buy stocks in several mining companies based in Texas, and I did. Over several months, he gave me more tips, and because he'd been right the previous time I took his advice."

"How much was his cut?" Duane asked.

Roderick hung his head. "Twenty grand per transaction."

A cold chill stabbed Morrison's spine, and sweat drenched his white Nike T-shirt. He knew where the story was going, what Roderick and his colleague had done, and wanted to know how his brother could have been so stupid, so greedy. Their parents had given him everything he'd ever wanted, but it was never enough for him. After graduating from college, their parents had given them each five million dollars to invest with. Within two years, Morrison had doubled his money, but Roderick had nothing to show for it—except a money-hungry fiancée with champagne tastes. A full-time diva, with no career aspirations, Toya spent her days shopping and tweeting and bragging on her social media pages about her glamorous lifestyle.

Morrison recalled the article he'd read about the Janssen family months earlier. Page Six reported that Simeon and Danika Janssen had lost everything after a series of bad investments, but Toya told Roderick the *New York*

Post was wrong, claimed her family was still worth billions. Morrison didn't believe her. If they were wealthy, why was she living off Roderick? Why didn't she have any credit cards or properties in her name? Why did his brother have to support her financially? Cute, but hard to please, Morrison didn't understand why his brother was smitten with her. Toya was demanding, and the only person in their family who liked her was Roderick.

"His wife dropped by the office on Friday, and that's when I discovered she's a corporate lawyer working on several lucrative deals involving mining companies," Roderick explained in a grave voice. "Connor got the information from his wife, but knew he couldn't buy the stocks himself, so he used me to do it and like a fool I fell for his scheme."

"Has your colleague or his wife been arrested?" Duane asked.

"No, not yet, but Connor's scared out of his mind, and talking crazy. Yesterday, he told me he's going to resign, clear out his bank accounts and head to Europe until things die down."

Morrison asked the question at the forefront of his mind, and hoped for his brother's sake that his profit on the stock exchange was minimal. "How much money did you make?"

A proud grin filled his mouth. "One point six million dollars. It's enough to pay for the wedding, our honeymoon in Ibiza and matching his-and-her Ferraris."

"Does Toya know what's going on?"

The light in his eyes dimmed, and his demeanor changed, grew dark.

"She told me to keep my mouth shut, and if the cops question me to deny everything…"

Of course she did, Morrison thought, disgusted. *Toya*

will do anything for money. "You better not," Duane
warned, giving his brother a shot in the arm. "The Securities Exchange and Commission is no joke, and if you
lie to investigators you could be charged with obstruct-
ing justice."

"Or worse, end up in jail." Morrison couldn't imagine
anything worse than being confined to a six-by-eight cell,
and knew if Roderick was arrested his parents would be
devastated. "If Martha Stewart can get jail time for lying
to investigators, anyone can, so you have to be smart, or
the judge will make an example of you in court."

Releasing a deep sigh, his shoulders bent, Roderick
stared out at the morning sky.

"I feel like my life is spiraling out of control, and
there's nothing I can do to stop it."

"This is what you're going to do," Morrison advised in
a stern voice. He had to get through to Roderick, needed
his brother to understand the gravity of the situation.
He'd traded on the stock exchange, after receiving con-
fidential information from his colleague, and there was
only one way to make things right. "First, you're going
to tell Mom and Dad what's going on. Then, we'll meet
with investigators at the SEC, tell them the truth and
repay the money."

Roderick slowly nodded his head. "I, ah, guess I could
do that."

"Lastly, you'll check yourself into a rehab facility to
get clean and sober."

"A rehab facility?" Roderick repeated, shouting his
words. "I don't need rehab."

"Yes, you do. Your drinking has gotten out of hand,
and we're worried about you."

"Just because I smoke a little weed from time to time

and down a few beers after a hard day's work doesn't mean I have a problem. I don't."

"You can go somewhere discreet, and no one will ever have to know where you went," Duane said. "You don't have to do it alone, Roderick. We'll do it together."

"I—I—I can't go right now," he stammered, shuffling his feet. "There's a lot going on…"

His excuses were endless, but his brothers didn't back down, wouldn't let him talk his way out of attending a treatment facility out of state.

"When?" Duane pressed. "Give us a date, right here, right now."

Seconds passed, then what felt like minutes, but Roderick didn't speak. He dropped down onto the bench, closed his eyes and rubbed his face with his hands.

"We're not returning to shore until you tell us when you're going to rehab."

"I can't take time off work. My clients can't survive a week without me, let alone a month," he argued, lines wrinkling his forehead. "And what about Toya? Our wedding is right around the corner. She needs me to help finalize the details."

Duane disagreed. "No, you need to take care of yourself. Everything else can wait."

Morrison felt his cell phone vibrating in his pocket, and even though he was anxious to hear from Karma, he didn't retrieve his cell, wanted to give Roderick his undivided attention.

"Fine," he said with a pensive expression on his face, his voice resigned. "I'll meet with the SEC in May, after Memorial Day, then I'll go to treatment."

"You're making the right choice," Duane said. "I'm proud of you, bro."

Releasing the breath he'd been holding, Morrison ruffled Roderick's short, black hair. "So am I, and I'll do everything in my power to help you."

Chapter 11

"Who is *that* in the navy pinstripe suit?" the statuesque masseuse asked, wetting her peach lips with her pierced tongue. "Damn, he's so fine I want to have his babies!"

All of the women at the bar cheered and giggled, but Karma didn't turn around. Knew the masseuse was all talk, would rather build her mobile, esthetician business than find true love. They'd met at Networking After Dark months earlier, and every week the brunette sang the same tune. She'd meet a guy, take him home, then complain when he didn't call her for a second date. Karma didn't understand why the Miami native with the high IQ didn't smarten up and quit letting men use and mistreat her, but she kept her opinion to herself. They were acquaintances, not besties, and Karma didn't want to ruffle anyone's feathers.

"I do business with musicians, athletes, Bollywood stars and even Oscar winners…"

Tasting her margarita, Karma blocked out the raucous noise at the bar and listened to what the hedge fund manager was saying about his famous clients. Didn't want to miss a word. Committed everything he said to memory. Not because he was charismatic or entertaining, because Karma was determined to take Beauty by Karma to the next level, and it started with having rich, influential friends. She'd made a point of not only introducing herself to everyone at the event, but also handing out business cards and connecting with like-minded professionals.

The Palm East Hampton was the quintessential New York steak house, and the lively crowd, and club-like atmosphere, made the restaurant one of the best places to eat on the island. The courteous staff, celebrity sightings and outstanding wine list attracted diners from all over the state, and every week Karma looked forward to attending Networking After Dark at her favorite Hamptons bar.

Animated conversation and boisterous laughter filled the air, and the lounge was so crowded Karma couldn't move without bumping into someone, but she was in no rush to go home. Wanted to mingle and socialize for hours more. She'd been working like a dog all week, and she deserved to relax and unwind.

Feeling her cell vibrate inside her clutch purse, Karma took it out of the side pocket and punched in her password. Raising an eyebrow, she tapped her fingernail against her cell phone case. She had three new text messages from Morrison, and reading them made her giggle. He was as charming as he was persistent, but Karma didn't respond to his messages. Knew if she did they'd end up back in bed, and two people with strong personalities had no business being together—not even for one night. In his message, he'd asked her to have a drink with him, but Karma knew what Morrison wanted, and she wasn't going to fall for his smooth speech.

"I have two tickets to see *Star Wars the Musical*, and I want you to be my date."

The hedge fund manager asked for her number, and Karma wore a polite smile. He smelled of Vicks Vapo-Rub, and she wasn't sexually attracted to him, but she searched inside her purse for a business card. Finding one, Karma handed it to him and waved goodbye.

"He's exactly my type," the masseuse proclaimed. "And I have to meet him."

Karma glanced over her shoulder, searching the lounge for the man in the navy pinstripe suit who'd caught the masseuse's eye. Morrison raised his glass in the air, and a sly grin claimed his mouth. Her heartbeat sped up. She hadn't been the same since the day he'd stormed into her salon, slinging insults, and sleeping with him only intensified her feelings. Made her desire him more.

Morrison beckoned her over with a flick of his head, but she didn't move. Stayed put. Dodged his gaze. The masseuse squealed, cheered so loud Karma feared she'd have permanent hearing loss in her right ear, and shot the brunette a what-the-hell-is-wrong-with-you look. Of course. The masseuse thought Morrison was flirting with her, and maybe he was.

"Don't go over there," Karma warned. "Trust me, you're too much woman for Judge Morrison Drake. He prefers quiet, docile types he can control, not strong, accomplished women with ideas and opinions, who think for themselves."

"His name is Morrison?" Her almond-shaped eyes widened. "What a sexy name!"

"Don't do it. I know what I'm talking about."

"*Someone* sounds bitter," the masseuse replied. "What happened? You made a move on him, and he shot you down, huh?"

Karma shrugged a shoulder. "Okay, but don't say I didn't warn you."

"Warn me?" Laughing long and hard, as if she was watching an episode of *Modern Family*, the masseuse stuck out her chest and flipped her long, lush curls over her shoulders. "I'm not trying to be conceited, but look at me. I'm impossible to resist."

"Just so you know, Morrison cares more about a woman's personality than her physical appearance," Karma said.

"Is that right? For someone who doesn't like him, you sure know a lot about him."

"His niece works part-time at my salon, and I've, um, talked to him a few times."

You've done a lot more than talk! quipped her inner voice.

"I think you should go over there and show us how it's done, *Ms. Personality.*"

Karma faked a laugh. "As if! You're the one lusting over him, Chrissy, not me."

"Put your money where your mouth is," she challenged, propping her hands on her hips. "I bet a hundred bucks you won't get his number, but I will."

"A hundred bucks?" Karma repeated, twirling an index finger in the air. "Girl, please. That's chump change. Make it a thousand and you're on."

All at once, the women opened their designer purses and placed their bets. To Karma's surprise, everyone put their money on Chrissy. *If they only knew!* Karma thought, as memories of her passionate night with him filled her mind. *I've done things with Morrison that would make a dominatrix blush!*

"Go on, girl. Go over there and wow Morrison with your stellar personality."

Karma was so busy trash-talking with Chrissy she didn't notice Morrison come up behind her, until he slid an arm around her waist and kissed her cheek. Caught off guard, Karma gasped. She didn't know why Morrison was holding her close, or gazing into her eyes, but she figured it was for the masseuse's benefit and returned his smile. The expression on his face put her at ease, and his touch gave goose bumps.

"Good evening, ladies," he said with a polite nod. "What are you betting on?"

The masseuse smirked. "That Karma won't get your number."

"I hope you didn't bet against her, because she already has it. Now if you'll excuse us, ladies, Karma and I need to speak in private."

Eyes widened and jaws dropped when Morrison clasped Karma's hand and shouldered his way through the crowd. Always smooth, never in a hurry, his calm, unflappable nature was a turn-on, and for a moment, Karma forgot she was mad at him. Wished they were at her place, instead of at the noisy, jam-packed lounge. Morrison led her through the bar, out the front door of the restaurant and into the parking lot.

Chilly, Karma wrapped her arms around her bare shoulders. Stars dotted the night sky, the evening breeze ruffled the tree branches, and the air smelled of cigarette smoke. It was late, time for Karma to get home to bed, but she wanted to hear what Morrison had to say. Was Reagan in trouble again? Were her grades slipping? Was he there to ask her to fire his niece again?

Opening the back door of his Bentley, Morrison stepped aside and gestured for Karma to get inside. She shook her head. Knew if she got in all bets were off, and the last thing she wanted was to lose control in his car. "No, thanks. I'm fine right here."

Morrison leaned forward, and his cologne fell over her. Her mouth watered.

"That's some outfit, Karma."

"I know, right?" she said with a laugh, doing a twirl. She'd paired the strapless dress with a floral clutch and ankle-tie pumps, and from the time she'd arrived at The Palm East Hampton other patrons had been complimenting her look. "I bought it yesterday at my favorite boutique, and I love it."

"As you should be. You look sensational, but that's no surprise. You always do."

Karma raised an eyebrow. "You didn't bring me out here to discuss my remarkable fashion sense, so what's up?" she asked, anxious to get to the bottom of things. "What are you doing here? You're not a small business owner."

"I came to see you, of course. What do I have to do to fix things?"

"What are you taking about? Fix what?"

"Fix us," he said in a somber voice. "You're avoiding me."

"Avoiding you? Morrison, don't be ridiculous. I've been busy with the salon."

"Too busy to take my calls? I phoned you last night but you never got back to me."

"I didn't get home from my date until midnight, and I figured it was too late to call."

His gaze narrowed, and the expression on his face was hostile, but his tone was calm.

"Do you go on blind dates every night?"

"God no," Karma quipped, shivering at the thought. "I tried online dating a few times, but each date was worse than the last. And the mama's boy from Queens, who conveniently forgot his wallet at home—after insisting we have dinner at the most expensive sushi restaurant in the city—has me seriously considering a vow of celibacy for the rest of my thirties!"

Morrison chuckled, and the sound of his hearty laughter tickled her eardrums, made her smile. Brought to mind all the times they'd flirted and joked around on her birthday. Her gaze lingered on his mouth, and she imagined herself ravishing his lips, ripping the designer suit from his body and kissing him all over. Try as she might, she couldn't escape her explicit thoughts. Karma was glad Morrison couldn't read her mind, because if he did they wouldn't be chatting about the pitfalls of online dating, they'd be making out.

"Are you working tomorrow evening?" Morrison asked.

"I'm *always* working," she said with a laugh, leaning against his gleaming white car. "I want Beauty by Karma to be the premier salon in the Hamptons, and I'm willing to do anything to make it happen, including making house calls and working eighty hours a week."

"We're having dinner at Masa tomorrow night and I won't take no for an answer."

Stunned, Karma raised an eyebrow. "How did you get a reservation at the best restaurant in New York City? You must have friends in high places, because I have clients who've been on the waiting list for years."

"You've been giving me the cold shoulder all week, so I had to do something big to win you over, and nothing says I think you're special like an extravagant meal at Masa."

"Sorry, Morrison, but I have to work." Karma wore a sad smile, but deep down she was glad her schedule was packed. The more she worked, the less time she had to think about her mother's death, her attraction to Morrison and her problems with Jazz. "It's always super busy at the salon, and with three stylists off we need all hands on deck."

"All work and no play makes Karma a dull girl," he joked. "Sound familiar?"

Karma faked a frown. "I'm not dull. I'm fabulous, and don't you forget it!"

"That's why I want to date you. You're unlike anyone I've ever met, and I want us to be exclusive," he confessed, stepping forward. "I don't want anyone else but you."

"Exclusive? After one night together? Morrison, that's crazy—"

He cupped her chin in his hand, and the knot in her stomach tightened.

"No, what's crazy is that you actually think you can resist me."

His confidence was a turn-on, made Karma want to devour his mouth.

"I'm a Drake, Karma. I don't let anything stop me from achieving my goals, and right now I have my sights set on you, so quit playing hard to get. It's not going to work."

Stepping back, she folded her arms across her chest. "I'm not a conquest, Morrison."

"That's right. As of today you're my girl, and I don't want you hooking up with guys on online dating apps, like that cheapskate from Queens, or Tiago Van den Berg."

"Oh, so that's why you're here," she said in a sing-song voice. "You heard I went sailing with Tiago Van den Berg, and you're jealous."

"You deserve better. He isn't good enough for you."

"And you are?"

"Absolutely. I'm the perfect man for you, and I proved it your birthday weekend."

Heat flooded her cheeks, and her erect nipples strained against her lace bra.

"Morrison, I don't think we should date," she said, ignoring her tingling body.

"Why? Because we argued at Cove Lounge?"

"No, because we clash."

A grin curled his mouth. "Not in the bedroom. We're totally in sync."

"Just because we had amazing, toe-curling sex a few times doesn't mean we'll have a successful relationship. We're both stubborn, headstrong people. It'll never work."

His eyes brightened, and his smile was as broad as his shoulders. "I made your toes curl? Well, I'll be damned. I didn't know I put it down like *that*."

Hearing noises behind her, Karma glanced over her shoulder. Patrons spilled out of the restaurant, and hip-hop music blared from the silver SUV parked beside the lamppost. Karma opened her mouth to tell Morrison she was leaving, but he stepped forward and her breath caught in her throat. Her thoughts were muddled because of his closeness, and the scent of his cologne. Part of her wanted to leave, to put some distance between them, but another part of her—a bigger part of her—wanted to stay.

"The way I see it, you have two choices." Morrison pulled her to his chest and dropped his mouth to her ear. "You can have dinner with me at Masa, or we can hang out together at the salon, but make no doubt about it, I'm seeing you tomorrow night, so what will it be?"

His words, and the defiant expression on his face, caught Karma off guard, and for the second time in minutes she struggled to speak, didn't know what to say in response to his question. "Morrison, it's wedding season, my busiest time of the year," she explained, finding her voice. "And if I want to be *the* stylist to the stars I have to be available to my clients 24/7."

"Fine, I'll bring some food to the salon and keep you company while you work."

"No!" she shouted, shaking her head at his outrageous suggestion. "I'll reschedule my seven o'clock appointment so we can have dinner at Masa."

Morrison winked. "Cool. I thought you'd see things my way."

He sounded pleased with himself and his wide, I'm-the-man grin made Karma remember the first time they'd made love. They'd laughed and played in bed, and although they hadn't known each other long she'd felt close to him, as if he'd genuinely cared about her and her feelings. Not to mention, he'd pleased her sexually. In ways she'd never imagined.

"Beautiful moments can't be planned, only experienced..." Morrison said in a smooth voice.

Karma never saw the kiss coming, told herself if she did she would have moved out of the way, but when Morrison's lips touched hers, she sank against his chest, desperate for more.

Morrison unlocked the front door of his newly renovated East Lake estate, turned off the security alarm and tossed his keys on the glass console table. One of his mother's former employees, an impeccably dressed interior designer with a penchant for silk ties and top hats, had decorated his mansion with Italian marble, lush colors and fabrics, and the souvenirs he'd collected during his travels around the world. At Reagan's urging, he'd transformed the den into a home theater with custom seating and mood lighting, and now it was Morrison's favorite room in the house. He'd been so pleased with the renovations he'd given the designer a bottle of Hennessy and a five-figure bonus.

Morrison headed into the kitchen to fix himself a snack. Whistling the Bruno Mars song Karma had played for him earlier at her condo, he bobbed his head, and snapped his fingers. Morrison felt on top of the world, as if he was eighteen again.

A grin filled his mouth. After kissing Karma in the parking lot of The Palm East Hampton, he'd followed her to her condo so they could "talk," but the moment they entered the dimly lit foyer he'd made his move. Overcome with passion, he'd devoured her mouth. Kissing her, he'd unzipped her dress, took off her undergarments and tossed them aside. They'd made love on the couch, and hours later he was still thinking about their frenzied lovemaking. No one had ever done the things to him that Karma did—licked from his earlobes to his nipples, sandwiched his erection between her breasts then eagerly sucked it, encouraged him to switch positions to prolong their lovemaking—and her sexual prowess blew his mind.

But what made Karma stand out from all the other women he'd dated was her personality. How real and authentic she was, how much she loved her clients, her employees, and her family and friends. Their lovemaking was exhilarating, but what he'd enjoyed most was holding her in his arms afterward, discussing anything and everything that came to mind. Karma loved to talk, and debate, and joke around, and said things that challenged his way of thinking. In many ways, she reminded him of

Emmanuelle, and spending time with her was a welcome reprieve from his busy, demanding life.

The lights came on in the kitchen, blinding him, and Morrison stopped abruptly. Reagan was sitting on the counter, clutching her cell phone in her hands, scowling at him. "It's one a.m." she said, folding her arms across her chest. "Where have you been?"

Morrison frowned. "Why are you still up? You should be in bed. You have calculus first period, and a midterm exam in world history you need to be well rested for."

"I'm the one asking the questions, mister, not you."

Amused by the stern expression on her face, and her no-nonsense tone, he hid a smile.

"You were supposed to come to the graduation information session tonight at Hampton Academy, but you were a no-show. What's up with that?"

Filled with guilt, Morrison hung his head, couldn't believe he'd forgotten about the meeting at his niece's private school, and wished there was something he could do to make it up to her. "Honey, I'm sorry. It slipped my mind."

"I called your cell like a hundred times, but you didn't answer."

"I forgot my cell in the car, and when I tried to turn it on it was dead."

"Likely story," she quipped, rolling her eyes to the ceiling. "How convenient."

"I'll be at the next meeting. I promise."

"What's going on with you? You rarely go out on weekdays, and if you do you're always home at supper time."

"I went to a networking event that ran late, but I'll make sure this doesn't happen again," Morrison said with an apologetic smile, taking her hand in his and squeezing it.

"It better not, or I'll tell Grandma Viola and she'll ground you for a month."

Morrison chuckled. "Time for bed, kiddo. You have to be up early tomorrow—"

"Did you have fun with Ms. Karma?" Reagan asked, hopping off the counter.

"How did you know I was with Ms. Karma?"

Smirking, she pointed a finger at his face. "I didn't. *You* just told me!"

Mad at himself for falling for the oldest trick in the book, Morrison inwardly scolded himself.

"You like her a lot, don't you?"

"Yeah," he confessed, deciding it was time to come clean to his niece about his feelings for her boss. "She's fun, down-to-earth, and I enjoy hanging out with her."

"I told you Ms. Karma was amazing." Reagan opened the freezer, took the container of chocolate ice cream off the bottom shelf and slammed the door shut with her foot. "Why don't you invite her over next Sunday for lunch? We can have a barbecue, so the whole family can meet her. Grandma would love that. You know how anxious she is for you to settle down, and give her some grandbabies."

To make his niece laugh, he joked, "We've only been on a few dates. It's too soon. Besides, I don't want Toya and Roderick to scare her off. You know they're extra."

Giggling, she opened the cupboard and grabbed two oversize ceramic bowls.

"Not so fast, young lady." Morrison plucked the ice cream container out of his niece's hands, returned it to the freezer and steered her out of the kitchen. "It's time for bed. You have a full day ahead of you tomorrow, and so do I."

Climbing the staircase to the second floor together, Reagan filled Morrison in on the graduation information session, her exam schedule and her increased hours at Beauty by Karma in May. Something Karma had said about Reagan days earlier came to mind, and Morrison wondered if it was true. "Are you having second thoughts about becoming a lawyer?"

"I love doing hair and makeup too, and Ms. Karma thinks I have real talent."

"Fine, practice on your friends and classmates at Hampton Academy, but you're going to New York University in the fall, and that's final. Have I made myself clear?"

"What about what I want? Don't I deserve to be happy?"

"Of course, but doing hair and makeup is beneath you. You're a Drake, Reagan. *A Drake*," he repeated, stressing his words. "I won't stand by and watch you ruin your life. You're going to college, not beauty school. I forbid it—"

"I don't care what you think. It's my decision to make, not yours. Ms. Karma believes in me and, most importantly, I believe in myself."

For a moment, Morrison was speechless. Couldn't get a word out. Reagan never raised her voice to him, let alone yelled, and he didn't appreciate her tone. Wasn't going to stand for her disrespectful attitude. "If you ever speak to me like that again you'll lose more than just your car," he said, meeting her narrowed gaze. "This conversation is over. Now go to bed."

"I'm sick and tired of you telling me what to do. Maybe I should go live with Uncle Roderick and Toya for the rest of the school year. They understand me better, and…"

Over my dead body! Morrison thought, vigorously shaking his head. *You're not going anywhere. This is your home, and I'm your legal guardian. More important, I love you, and I'd be lonely if you weren't here.* "Reagan, this isn't open for discussion. You cannot be a stylist. You made plans for the future, and you're going to see them through."

Sniffing, tears shimmering in her eyes, Reagan stomped into her bedroom, slammed the door in Morrison's face and blasted her stereo.

Chapter 12

"I have a bad feeling about this." Karma was sweating profusely in her ruffled, polka-dot bathing suit, but she tried not to let her nervousness show. Didn't want Morrison to know she was afraid. Wanted him to think she was adventurous and youthful, like the other women frolicking on Coopers Beach, but she had knots in her stomach. "I've never gone kayaking before, and I don't want to embarrass myself. Or worse, end up in a neck brace."

"Baby, don't worry. I've got you. I won't leave your side."

Leaning over, Morrison pressed his lips to her mouth. Closing her eyes, Karma snuggled against his chest, reveled in the beauty of the moment. His smile was his best feature, what dazzled her every time, but it was his kiss that made her weak. He was the most amazing man she'd ever met, and Karma treasured their time together. She was exhausted, beat after working five consecutive twelve-hour shifts, but she'd rather spend the day with Morrison at the beach than catch up on sleep. Since Networking After Dark, they'd had dinner at Masa, played doubles tennis with his brother and sister-in-law, and watched movies at her condo. They'd been dating for three weeks, and every day Karma found something new to love about Morrison. He was the most honorable, selfless man she knew, and she adored him.

Voices filled the air, shattering the silence, and Karma dropped her hands to her sides. Coopers Beach, a seven-mile stretch of soft, powder-white sand along the Atlantic shoreline, was Karma's favorite hangout spot, and the most beautiful beach in the Hamptons. Hundreds of yards wide, there was ample space to play Frisbee and volleyball, and build sandcastles. Packed with families, teenagers and couples, it was a popular hangout spot on the weekends, and because of the A-list stars sunbathing, Coopers Beach was crawling with paparazzi.

"Let's get out there. The sky's clear, the water's cool and the sun is hot," Morrison pointed out, affectionately patting her hips. "No time like the present, right?"

"I'm right behind you," she said. "Lead the way."

The water was calm, but cold, and Karma shivered as she dragged the small, yellow kayak from the sand to the shore. *The things we do for love!* Her heart stopped, and perspiration wet her skin. Shaking her head, Karma dismissed the thought. Sure, she and Morrison had a strong bond, and mind-blowing chemistry, but they hadn't been dating long, and she'd be a fool to think they'd last forever. They wouldn't. Couldn't. It was a fling, and nothing more, and by the time the summer ended, she'd probably be a distant memory to him. And that suited Karma just fine. She couldn't risk him discovering the truth about her past, and shuddered to think what would happen to her business if her well-heeled clients found out about her family. Karma emptied her mind, refused to think about the worst day of her life.

"I'll help you get in," he said, moving toward her. "It's harder than it looks."

"Morrison, I'm fine. This is the easy part, it's the sharks I'm worried about!"

After sliding the kayak into the water, with the bow first as Morrison had advised her minutes earlier, Karma placed her hand on the stern, holding it in place. Taking a deep breath to steady her nerves, she put one leg into the kayak, then the other. Tipping it toward her, she slid her butt onto the seat. Without warning, the boat tipped over, sending her crashing headfirst into the water. Mortified, Karma shot to her feet and wiped at her eyes.

Out of her peripheral vision, she saw teenagers on the shore, pointing and laughing, and winced. The water was shallow, only reaching her knees, and Karma felt like an imbecile for falling out of the boat. That's what she got for agreeing to go kayaking with Morrison, even though she'd never tried it before. He'd arrived at her condo early that morning, and after they'd had breakfast on the patio they'd driven down to Coopers Beach for some fun in the sun. Now Karma regretted her decision.

"Are you okay? You didn't hurt yourself, did you?"

At her side, Morrison spoke to her in a calm, soothing voice. Wearing a concerned expression on his face, he tenderly rubbed her neck and shoulders. Seeing the compassion in his eyes made her feel foolish and clumsy. "I told you this was a bad idea," she complained. "I don't know anything about kayaks."

"Don't sweat it. I'll teach you everything I know." Morrison kissed the tip of Karma's nose. "By the time we finish our first lap around you'll be a pro."

"Our first lap?" she repeated, her voice shrill. "How many laps are we doing? I'm a novice, Morrison. You have to take it easy on me. I'm a kayak virgin."

He chuckled, and the sound of his hearty belly laugh made her giggle too.

"When you're ready to quit just say the word and we'll head back to shore."

Karma clutched Morrison's outstretched hand and climbed into the kayak. Sitting upright, with her feet flat and her legs against the thigh braces, Karma took her sunglasses off her head and put them on. Feeling more confident after her pep talk from Morrison, she grabbed her paddle, eager to put his advice to the test, and slowly rotated her arms.

"You're holding it backward. The smooth side of the paddle should be facing you."

"I knew that," Karma said, flipping it over, and flashing a seductive smile. "I was testing you. I wanted to make sure you were paying attention."

"Karma, when it comes to you I'm *always* paying attention."

Seconds later, they were off, their kayaks moving slowly side by side in the water. The sun was bright and warm, the sky a vibrant shade of blue. Butterflies danced around them, a refreshing scent filled the air, and the tranquil atmosphere made Karma feel peaceful, more content than she'd been in months. Initially, she'd been leery about taking the day off work to go kayaking with Morrison, but Karma was glad she'd accepted his invitation. She enjoyed being outdoors, surrounded by nature, and was having fun at Coopers Beach. Bustling with activity, the beach was filled with surfers, swimmers, gleaming yachts and Jet Skis.

"This is my definition of heaven, and being here brings back great memories," Morrison said with a pensive expression on his face. "This used to be Emmanuelle's favorite beach, and we spent a lot of time here when we were teens. We'd pig out at the concession stand, play volleyball for hours and surf until dark."

"Does losing someone you love ever get easier? Every morning I wake up, and still can't believe my mom is gone. She was my best friend and now life feels empty without her."

"I don't think grief gets any easier. You just learn how to cope better."

Karma leaned forward in her seat. Beneath the surface of the crystal-clear water, she noticed sea otters, seals, porpoises, and wished she had her iPhone with her to capture the image. "It's so beautiful out here. I should have brought my cell with me to take pictures."

A frown darkened his face. "I'm glad you left it in the car. It rings nonstop."

"You're just jealous because I have more friends than you," she joked, smirking.

"No, your clients are selfish and demanding, and they're constantly taking advantage of you. If I had my way you'd work eight hours a day, no evenings or weekends."

Karma pretended not to hear him. She didn't say anything for fear they'd end up arguing again about her work schedule. The sun felt warm against her skin, and the breeze whipped her loose curls at her face. Her stomach groaned, but eating was the last thing on her mind.

Resting her paddle on her lap, she took a moment to soak in the beauty and serenity around her. There was something magical about being in the middle of the ocean, listening to the sounds of nature. It was an indescribable feeling, one she'd never forget. The kayak drifted aimlessly along the water, and when Morrison offered to tow her back to shore Karma laughed.

"Karma, I need you…"

I need you too. His smile aroused her flesh, made her yearn for him. It wasn't the time or the place to put the moves on Morrison, but Karma shot him a sultry stare, wanted him to know how much she desired him. It wasn't just his breathtaking French kisses or the outstanding sex; it was his heart, his character, and although Karma would never admit it to anyone she'd been smitten with him from the moment she'd first laid eyes on him. She couldn't think of anything better than being with Morrison, and when they returned to shore she was dragging him back to his BMW for a quickie.

"I'm thinking of throwing a surprise graduation party for Reagan in June, and I need someone with your skill and expertise to help me plan it," he explained, his expression hopeful. "I know you're crazy busy right now with the salon, but it would mean a lot if you could give me a hand with the menu, theme and decorations."

"Morrison, that's so sweet. Reagan's going to be stoked!" Full of ideas, Karma cheered, couldn't contain her excitement. "Say no more. I'm in. Anything you need, just ask. Reagan's like a little sister to me, and I'll do anything for her."

"Thanks, Karma, I knew I could count on you."

His voice was full of emotion, and his words touched her heart.

"I told you you'd be good at kayaking," Morrison said, smiling. "You're a natural."

"You're right, this *is* fun. Who knew?"

Morrison glanced at his watch. "Ready to go to the Bay Kitchen Bar for lunch or do you want to do another lap around and take some pictures with my cell?"

"Lunch!" Karma said with a laugh, unable to hide her feelings. They hadn't been kayaking long, but her legs had fallen asleep and her arms were aching from paddling through the water. "And, we better hurry. My stomach is growling so loud I bet everyone on shore can hear it!"

An open, airy space, with a striking royal blue color scheme and a contemporary decor, the Bay Kitchen Bar had a beach vibe and a relaxed ambience. On the top floor of the Harbor Marina, the restaurant provided fine cuisine and stunning views of the harbor.

Sitting on the patio with Morrison, watching the world go by, Karma sipped her watermelon-flavored cocktail. *So much for losing weight for the Hamptons Women Association banquet in July,* she thought, helping herself to a coconut shrimp on the appetizer platter. *I've been so busy hanging out with Morrison I haven't seen my trainer in weeks!* Karma refused to feel guilty. She was with Morrison, and being with him made her feel like the luckiest woman alive.

Spicy aromas and spirited conversation drifted from the dining room to the deck. Every table in the restaurant was taken, the adjoining bar was packed, and the waiting area was filled with young, moneyed patrons, waiting anxiously to be seated.

"I need to ask you something, Karma..."

Morrison was wearing sunglasses, so Karma couldn't see his eyes, but she could tell by the tone of his voice and his stiff posture that something was bothering him.

"Did you pressure my niece to apply to beauty school?"

Shaking her head, Karma finished chewing the food in her mouth, and wiped her hands on the napkin draped across her lap. "No, Reagan came to me with a stack of applications a few days after she started working at the salon, and we discussed her options. I didn't convince her to do anything. It was all her doing, but I wholeheartedly support her decision and you should too."

Morrison released a deep sigh, as if the weight of the world was on his shoulders. "I wish you'd told me about this sooner. These days, all Reagan and I do is argue, and I'm frustrated by her cavalier attitude about school. She has a full scholarship to one of the best universities in the country, and I'm not going to let her throw away this incredible opportunity to do hair and makeup—"

"Being a stylist isn't a crappy, end-of-the road job, Morrison."

His eyes narrowed. "I never said it was."

"No, but you act like it is, and that couldn't be further from the truth."

"I'm sorry, I don't mean to. I'm just upset. I can't get through to Reagan."

"Would it be so bad if she went to beauty school?" Karma pressed. "I'm not an expert, and I don't have any kids, but isn't a parent supposed to love and support their child unconditionally? Thank God my mom did, or I never would have found my true passion. She believed in me, when no one else did, and I owe every success to her."

The waitress arrived with their entrées, set them on the wooden table, then left.

"You talk a lot about your mom, and your grandparents in Brooklyn, but you never speak about your dad. Why is that?"

"Because my aunt Charlene taught me never to speak ill of the dead."

Morrison picked up his fork. "Then, tell me your happiest memory of your dad."

"I don't have any."

"Come on, Karma. There must be one. I'm curious to know more about your relationship with your father."

Thinking hard, emotion clogged her throat, and a sad smile claimed her lips. "When I was nine, I went home for lunch, but my dad wasn't there to meet me. I returned to school, bawling my eyes out, my teacher Ms. Jenkins-Williams was nice enough to give me an apple…"

Morrison leaned forward in his chair, and Karma knew she had his attention.

"During story time, there was a knock on the class-room door, and in walked my dad with a McDonald's Happy Meal. He apologized for not being home at lunch, and I sat at my desk eating my fries. To this day, I still remember feeling incredibly special."

"It sounds like you had a great dad who loved you very much."

"I didn't. He was angry, and bitter, and I never un-derstood why my mom stayed with him." Karma was shocked by her admission, but wanted to open up to Mor-rison about her tumultuous relationship with her father. Wanted him to understand that his actions could have a negative effect on Reagan, and ultimately drive her away. "I asked my mom once, after she'd kicked my dad out for blowing our rent money at the local pool hall, and she looked at me in surprise, and said, 'I could never di-vorce your father. He's family, and you never, ever give up on family.'"

"Your mother was very wise," he said, slowly nodding his head. "It took losing Emmanuelle for me to appreciate my loved ones, and now I'll never take them for granted."

Karma's cell phone buzzed, and she glanced down at the screen. Reading her newest text message, a grin ex-ploded onto her mouth, and excitement coursed through her veins. She wanted to break out in song, but maintained her composure. Karma wanted to tell Morrison that Reagan had received an acceptance letter to one of the top beauty schools in the state, but she knew he'd be upset, so she kept her mouth shut.

"What is it? Let me in on the secret. You're beaming, and I want to know why."

"Babe, I'll be right back." Karma dropped her napkin on the table and rose to her feet. "I need to make a quick call, but I promise I won't be long."

"Hurry up, beautiful." Grinning, he tapped the face of his gold wrist watch. "I'm timing you."

Marching through the patio toward the washrooms, Karma dialed Reagan's number and put her cell to her ear. The teen answered on the first ring, and she cheered. "Congratulations, Reagan! I'm *so* proud of you. I knew you'd get in."

"Thanks, Ms. Karma. I couldn't have done it without you."

Joining the line for the ladies' room, she hoped it moved quickly so she could continue her date. "Now what?" Karma asked, tapping her wedge-clad feet impatiently on the ground. "Are you going to beauty school in September, or university?"

"I'm going to do both. I'll go to university during the day, and take courses at Aveda Institute in the evenings. That way Uncle Morrison and my grandparents will be happy."

"Reagan, that's going to be hard."

"I can do it, Ms. Karma. I'm smart, determined and focused. I've got this."

Karma didn't want to dampen the teenager's spirits, because she knew how much Reagan wanted to please her family, but attending university and beauty school full-time was going to be taxing. Making a mental note to speak to Morrison again about his niece's future, she said, "I know, sweetie, and I believe in you. You're destined for greatness."

"I know, right?" Reagan giggled. "Some of us girls just have it like that!"

Ending the call seconds later, Karma peered around the women in front of her to see what the holdup was. She wanted to return to her entrée and her handsome date, and if her hands didn't have sauce on them she'd ditch the line and head back to her table.

"You Jezebel! Stay away from my husband!" a female voice shouted.

Curious to see who was yelling, Karma glanced over her shoulder in search of the shrill, high-pitched voice. A blonde in a strapless ivory dress, stood directly behind Karma with her eyes narrowed and her arms crossed. Mascara smeared her cheeks, and her nose was running. Either she'd been crying, or she'd been caught in a rainstorm.

"You think you can break up my happy home, but you can't. I won't let you."

Her mouth dried, and shame flooded her body. Morrison was married? No, no, it couldn't be, she thought, adamantly shaking her head. He lived with Reagan at his lavish East Hampton estate, and if he had a wife she'd know about it. On Wednesday they'd had dinner at his mansion, on Thursday they'd had drinks with his brother and sister-in-law, and on Friday she'd joined the family for movie night. The romantic comedy had been juvenile, filled with clichéd scenes and jokes, but Reagan and her friends had loved it, and Karma had enjoyed snuggling with Morrison in the back row. Another thought came to mind. Was Morrison legally separated? Was that why the blonde was up in her face? Because she wanted him back?

"Karma, what's going on? Is everything okay?"

Morrison appeared at her side. He rested a hand on her waist, but Karma shied away from his touch, didn't want anything to do with him if he was playing her. It wouldn't be the first time a man had hurt her, but it damn sure would be the last. If Morrison could deceive her, anyone could, but Karma refused to think the worst about the man she—

"Baby, talk to me," he pleaded. "Why are you mad? What did I do?"

Folding her arms across her chest, Karma hit him with a look. "You're married?"

"No, of course, not. If I was married I wouldn't be here with you."

"This woman says she's your wife."

"No, I didn't," the blonde snapped, wrinkling her nose. "I'm married to Lorenzo Cardozo, and if you think you can destroy my family you're mistaken, because I'll never give him up…"

Something clicked in Karma's mind, and the truth hit her. Who the blonde was, and why she was confronting her at the Bay Kitchen Bar. Yesterday at the shop, Jazz's iPhone had died, and she'd asked to use Karma's cell to call her mom. Or at least that's what her bestie had told her. She didn't want to out Jazz to Mrs. Cardozo, but she had to make it clear that she didn't want the woman's husband. People were staring at them, glaring openly at her, and she didn't want the other patrons to think less of her, or bad-mouth her beloved shop.

"Mrs. Cardozo, I don't know who your husband is, and I've never met him."

"Liar!" she shouted, jabbing a finger in Karma's chest. "You called his cell yesterday, and your number came up on his phone. That's how I was able to track you down."

Her pulse was racing, but Karma spoke in a calm voice. "I own a beauty salon, and sometimes my staff use my cell. One of them must have called your husband, because it wasn't me. I have a boyfriend, and he's all the man I need."

Right on cue, Morrison draped an arm around Karma's waist and held her close. "My baby's right," he said with a proud smile. "I'm quite the catch. Just ask my mom!"

Giggles filled the corridor, proof that the other female patrons were as enamored with Morrison as Karma was, and to prove to the blonde that he was her man she kissed him.

"I—I—I'm sorry," the blonde stammered, casting her gaze to the wooden floor. "I thought you were my husband's mistress, and I overreacted. I apologize for embarrassing you."

The woman left, the crowd in the corridor dissipated, and Karma released the breath she was holding. It had been the longest minute of her life, a scary, nerve-racking moment, but she felt empathy toward the Mrs. Cardozo, not anger, and purposed in her heart to talk some sense into Jazz.

"Baby, how about another cocktail?" Morrison proposed, rubbing her shoulders as he led her through the corridor and back outside to the patio. "You look like you could use one."

"Just one?" Karma cocked an eyebrow. "No, I could use *two*, so keep them coming!"

Chapter 13

"**P**ut some more blond streaks in the front," advised the Latina rap star. Seated in chair number one, she peered at her reflection in the oversize mirror, fluffing her spiral curls. "I want it to look full and lush for the awards show tonight, so keep at it…"

Karma disagreed, thought adding more extensions would overwhelm the rapper's thin face, but since the customer was always right she opened another pack of Diamond Virgin Hair, and held it up against her head. "Do you want one more row, or two?"

"Use the whole pack. I want rock star hair, *chiquita*!"

Customers laughed, the rapper's entourage fervently nodded their heads and Reagan snapped pictures of the queen of Spanish rap with her cell phone. Arriving at the salon an hour earlier, Karma had found the famed rapper in the waiting room, and had no choice but to drop her bags and get to work. According to one of the stylists, Jazz had called to say she was running late, but Karma knew her best friend wasn't coming to the salon. Last night, after the trophy wife cursed her out at the Bay Kitchen Bar, she'd called Jazz to tell her what happened, and even though her friend had apologized, Karma was still upset. They hadn't been on the same page for months, and she was tired of making excuses to her staff about Jazz. They needed to talk, and this time she wouldn't let her bestie play the friend card, would hold her accountable for her actions and unprofessional behavior at the salon.

Energized by the spirited discussion around her, Karma chatted and laughed with her staff and customers. Watching a mother and her teenage daughter peruse the nail color tower, cherished memories flooded her mind—trying out new recipes in the kitchen with her mom, giggling with Carmelita on the bus to Karma's piano lessons, their weekly hair and nail appointments at their favorite beauty salon in Queens—and sadness consumed her. In the blink of an eye, she'd lost everything, the most important person in her life, and six years later Karma was still struggling to cope with her mom's death.

"I can't go to the mayor's luncheon tomorrow. I'm having dimplant surgery."

Surfacing from her thoughts, Karma stared at the college student in the leopard-print blouse, white skinny jeans and suede booties. "What's that?"

"Duh," the redhead joked, poking a finger at her cheek. "Permanent dimples."

"Seriously? I've never heard of such a thing."

"Get with the times, Ms. Karma. Surgeons can do anything," she said with a cheeky smile. "My mom always says, if God didn't give it to you just go out and buy it, and I agree!"

"My physical imperfections are what make me *me* and I'd never want to change that."

"I'm with Karma." Swiveling her neck, Poppy slid her hands along her ample curves. "I'm a hundred percent natural and a hundred percent fabulous."

The front door chimed, and Karma glanced over her shoulder, curious to see who the new arrival was. Her next appointment wasn't for an hour, and once she was finished doing the rapper's hair Karma was going to her office to update her blog.

Yawning, Karma struggled to keep her eyes open.

Of course you're tired, scolded her inner voice. *All these late night dates and early morning appointments are taxing, and you're running yourself ragged.*

Morrison had called last night as Karma was getting ready for bed, and they'd ended up talking on the phone for hours. No subject was off-limits, and thinking about all of the sweet, heartfelt things he'd said about her brought a smile to her lips.

"Good morning, lovelies!" Jazz greeted, sashaying into the salon on red-heeled pumps.

Dressed in a white halter jumpsuit, she smiled and waved like a Miss Universe contestant as she breezed past the reception area. Blessed with exceptional beauty, the self-proclaimed fashionista had tanned skin, wavy brown hair and an A-plus body that made men of all ages gawk and drool. "If anyone needs me I'll be in the office preparing for the day."

Preparing for the day, my ass, Karma thought, forcing herself not to roll her eyes. *You won't be working; you'll be yapping on the phone with your very married boyfriend.*

"It's super long, but I can cut it if you want." Picking up the gold, vintage mirror from off the counter, Karma held it up for the rapper to see the back of her hair. "What do you think?"

"That I'm going to be the baddest chick at the Latin Entertainment Awards!" she shrieked, dancing around in her leather chair. "Thanks, *chiquita*! I love it."

"I aim to please. Good luck at the award show tonight. I hope you win."

Winking, a smirk curled her lips. "I will. You can bet on it."

Karma took her cell phone out of her pocket and pressed the Camera app. "Stand still. I need to take some pictures of your sexy new hairstyle for my blog."

Everyone wanted a photograph with the queen of Spanish rap, and several minutes passed before the staff returned to their stations, and the customers put away their iPhones.

"Reina, tenemos que irnos. Estamos atrasados..."

Stepping forward, the bearded man in the gray sweat suit dropped ten crisp hundred-dollar bills on the counter, then escorted the rap star through the salon and out the front door. Karma picked up the money and put it in her smock. Her work done, Karma told her staff she was taking a break, and headed down the hallway, massaging her aching hands.

What a day, she thought, rubbing her eyes with her fingertips. It was only ten o'clock, but Karma was beat, so tired all she could think about was going home to bed. Though she wouldn't. Canceling on her clients wasn't an option, and even though Karma was exhausted, she was excited about the four o'clock photoshoot for *Salon Today* magazine in Manhattan.

Her cell phone pinged, and Karma read her newest text message from Morrison.

Roses are red, violets are blue, you're so damn sexy, I want to do you!

A giggle tickled her throat and fell from her mouth. Morrison was the strong, silent type, but he definitely had a humorous side, and Karma enjoyed their playful banter. Wanting to hear his voice, she decided to call him from the privacy of her office and quickened her steps. Karma opened the door, and stopped abruptly. Jazz was asleep on the couch, curled up in a beige blanket, snoring softly. "Jazz," she hissed, shaking her shoulders. "Wake up."

Stirring, she opened her eyes and stretched her arms in the air. "What is it?"

"I don't pay you to sleep. I pay you to manage the salon."

"Why are you being salty? I've only been sleeping for a few minutes."

"You should be on the floor, tending to customers, helping the staff and promoting the hell out of the salon, not hiding out in the office taking a siesta twenty minutes into your shift."

Shrugging, Jazz wore a sheepish expression on her face. "What can I say? I had a late night."

"Funny, you couldn't come to work yesterday, but you had the energy to attend the Black and White Gala in Harlem last night. And don't try and deny it because I saw the pictures you posted online."

"I wasn't missing that gala for anything. That party was lit! The only thing that would have made the night better was meeting Mariah Carey in person, but Lorenzo thought the meet and greet was lame, so we left after dessert." Standing, Jazz fluffed her hair and adjusted her clothes. "I'm out of here. I have some errands to do before I meet my boo for lunch."

"Jazz, this has gone on long enough. Either you're going to work, and do the job I'm paying you incredibly well to do, or—"

"Or what," she shot back, moulding her hands to her hips.

Her deep, dark stare was chilling, but Karma showed

no fear. She was shocked by the bitterness in her best friend's voice, but she stepped forward, not back. "For the past few months, you've been selfish, irresponsible and self-absorbed, and I'm sick of it."

"I helped you build this salon from the ground up, and if it wasn't for me, and my celebrity connections, this place would be empty. I'm the *real* captain of this ship, not you."

Is she high? Bewildered by her friend's outrageous response, Karma frowned. Her emotions overwhelmed her, and for a moment she couldn't speak. Needed a minute to gather her thoughts. "Our staff are responsible for the staggering success of Beauty by Karma, not you. Half the time you're not here, and when you are here you're texting and gabbing on your cell."

"I quit. I don't need this crap, and I don't need you." Jazz stomped over to her desk, grabbed her tote bag off the wingback chair, then hurled magazines, pictures and notepads inside. "Lorenzo's going to divorce his wife and marry me, and when he does I'll buy my own beauty salon, and it'll be a hell of a lot better than this dump."

Pain stabbed Karma's heart, and water filled her eyes, but she wouldn't cry. If she could survive losing her mother, she could survive losing Jazz. And, if she was being honest with herself, Jazz had stopped being a friend months ago. Only now, she knew her bestie was jealous of her success and didn't wish her well. "Jazz, he's playing you. Why can't you see that?"

"Bye," she quipped, her jam-packed bag hanging from her wrist. "Have a nice life."

Karma wanted to tell Jazz to kiss her derriere, but remembered she was a mature, sophisticated woman, and decided to take the high road. "Jazz, I appreciate everything you've done the past eighteen months to help make

Beauty by Karma a success. I couldn't have done any of this without you, and I wish you nothing but the best in your future endeavors."

The office was so quiet, Karma could hear the wall clock ticking from across the room. She met Jazz's gaze, willing her not to leave. Not like this. Jazz was the first person she'd met when she moved to the Hamptons, and Karma couldn't imagine them not seeing each other anymore. She could find another manager for the salon, but losing Jazz as a friend was a painful blow. One that would take a long time to heal.

Without another word, Jazz sauntered out the door, and slammed it behind her.

Her cell phone rang, and Unknown Caller came up on the screen. Karma pressed the answer button, knowing it was Morrison calling from the private line at his office. She needed to vent about her argument with Jazz, and Morrison was the perfect person to open up to. "You'll never believe what happened—"

"This is a collect call from an inmate at Livingston Correctional Facility," said an automated female voice. "To accept this call from Feisal Leonard, please press one now."

No, no, no! Karma pressed the end button, and chucked her cell into her purse. Stunned, she dropped down into her leather chair, her mind racing, a knot the size of a baseball in her throat. Her heart was beating so loud it roared in her ears.

Taking several deep breaths, Karma tried to make sense of what had happened. How did Feisal get her cell number? Who gave it to him? What did he want from her? Karma weighed her options, deliberated over what to do. She considered telling Morrison her story and asking him for legal advice, but dismissed the thought. They had a powerful connection, and Karma adored him, but she didn't feel comfortable confiding in him about her past. Wasn't brave enough to bare her soul. No, she'd just have to handle the situation herself.

Her cell phone rang, and perspiration wet her skin. Facing her fears, Karma peered inside her handbag, and found her cell at the bottom. Her hands trembled, and her knees knocked together under the desk. Unknown Number, appeared on the screen, and Karma stared at her cell with disgust. Wanted to toss it out the window. It was bad enough Feisal had mailed three letters to the salon last week; now he was blowing up her cell phone too? It didn't matter how many times Feisal called her. She wasn't taking his call today, tomorrow or any other day, and nothing would ever change her mind.

Chapter 14

Morrison stood in front of the stainless steel stove in his kitchen, with his arms folded across his chest, listening to Karma diss his ideas for Reagan's graduation party in June. She was teasing him, giving him a hard time about his suggestions, but he was aroused, not annoyed, by her jokes. Pretty, in a figure-hugging, mustard dress, her long, toned legs on display, the only thought on his mind was making love to her, but Morrison knew it wasn't the right time or place, and exercised self-control. "Babe, you're wrong. Reagan's going to love it. You'll see."

"No offense, but a princess-themed graduation party is whack."

"Whack?" he repeated. "Says who?"

"Says me, and since I have the final say I'm nixing the pink decor too."

"All right, Martha Stewart Jr. What do you have in mind?"

"I'm glad you asked." Hopping off her stool at the marble center island, Karma grabbed her handbag from one of the chairs at the kitchen table, retrieved a leather-bound notebook and flipped it open. "The theme has to be unique to Reagan. Something that speaks to who she is, and what she's about."

"You mean *besides* spending my money faster than I can earn it?"

Their banter was playful, and her touch along his shoulder gave him an adrenaline rush—and an erection. Morrison was in the mood, couldn't think of anything better than making love to Karma, but since he didn't want Reagan to catch them in the act when she returned home from study group at the library, he opened the oven, took out the vegetarian lasagna and put it on top of the stove to cool down. "You know Reagan well, and I'm sure she'll love whatever you plan for the graduation party."

Hopefully as much as I love you. Thankful he hadn't revealed the truth, Morrison slammed his mouth shut. Needing a cold drink, he opened the wine fridge, grabbed a bottle of Zinfandel and filled two glasses. Morrison quickly downed his drink. From the time Karma had arrived at his estate they'd been planning the surprise party, but once they were done finalizing the details of the event they'd have lunch in the outside living room.

Morrison heard his cell phone ring on the counter, and knew from the Nas ringtone that it was his brother calling, but decided to let the call go to voice mail. Next Thursday, he was going with Roderick to meet with investigators at the SEC, and hoped his connections in the department came through for him. His brother was a great guy who'd made a mistake and deserved a second chance. And Morrison was going to make sure Roderick got it.

"This is going to be the best graduation party ever!" Talking with her hands, her excitement was evident by the light in her eyes, and the sound of her voice. "We have to go all out. Reagan deserves it. We'll get catered food, a photo booth and props, a live band, and the best decorations and champagne money can buy!"

"Champagne? No way. Reagan's underage, and so are her friends, so we can't let them drink any alcohol."

"Fine, I'll make my tasty tropical punch, and add just a splash of wine," Karma said, pinching two fingers together. "Surely, you can break the rules this one time."

Morrison shook his head. "I can't. It goes against everything I stand for."

"Oh, really?" Cocking her head to the right, she draped her arms around his neck and flicked her tongue against his ear. "You didn't mind breaking the rules on your boat, in the back seat of your Beemer, or at Cedar Point Park the other night…"

Shivers rocked his spine. Karma was his weakness, had been from the moment he'd laid eyes on her, and since their kayaking excursion at Coopers Beach, they'd been inseparable. They'd spent a romantic weekend at a cozy bed-and-breakfast in Montauk, went on several fishing excursions and wine tasting tours and enjoyed an afternoon at the best couple spa in Manhattan Memorial Day weekend. Karma was a fun-loving beauty who'd helped him find his spontaneous side, and every day with her was an exciting adventure. Morrison adored her, and he wasn't the only one. Reagan loved her, Duane thought she was mad cool, Erikah was obsessed with her style and fashion, and his nephews were already calling her "Auntie Karma."

Morrison thought about his plans for the weekend. He was having a dinner party at his estate, and was looking forward to showing Karma off to his friends and family. Though in the back of his mind he worried his parents wouldn't like his feisty new girlfriend. In theory, introducing her to his parents sounded like a good idea, but he feared the dinner would be a bust. Unlike the women he'd dated in the past, Karma didn't come from money, or have a prestigious, executive job, and he hoped his parents wouldn't mistreat her because of her humble background.

"You're a bad boy trapped in a judge's body," Karma teased. "And you love getting down and dirty, just like me."

Morrison shook off his concerns, cleared every doubt from his mind as his girlfriend stroked his chest through his short-sleeve denim shirt. With Karma, he never knew what to expect, and it was damn hot. One day, it was a quickie in the shower, the next it was sex in an elevator. It didn't matter where they hooked up; the sex was always outstanding. More exhilarating than a roller coaster ride, and Morrison was addicted. So desperate for her, he couldn't resist sliding his hands under her dress and stroking her bottom.

"That's what makes us so good together," she continued. "Our ability to live in the moment, regardless of where we are, is what makes our lovemaking magical. And hot."

Morrison dropped his mouth to hers. "I want to bend you over the kitchen table, hike up your dress and bury myself deep inside you."

Smirking, she batted her long, thick eyelashes. "What's stopping you?"

"I'm weak for you, Karma. You're all I think about, all I want, the only one for me…" He broke off speaking, couldn't believe the words that had come out of his mouth. Morrison heard the longing in his voice, the vulnerability, and wanted to slap himself for acting desperate. He was, but he didn't want Karma to know he'd fallen hard for her. Wanted to wait until they'd been dating for a six months before he confessed his true feelings. Didn't want to scare her off by dropping the *L* bomb too soon.

"*Please* tell me you remembered to buy the tickets this morning," Karma said, undoing the buttons on his shirt, pressing her lips against his neck. "I promised Reagan I'd get her tickets for the Bruno Mars concert next month, but I was swamped at the salon."

"How could I forget? Reagan texted me a hundred times, and so did you!"

Karma wore an apologetic smile. "Sorry, babe, I wasn't trying to be a nag."

"I know. Good news. I got four front-row seats, so we can chaperone Reagan's date."

"You give new meaning to the term *doting uncle*," she quipped with a laugh.

"I'm just glad I got the tickets. You were right. Reagan's worked really hard this term, the whole year actually, and she deserves a night out on the town."

"Exactly!" Karma kissed his lips. "I love when you quote me. It's such a turn-on—"

A chime echoed throughout the house, and Karma trailed off speaking.

"If we're lucky, they'll get tired of waiting and go away," she said with a sly wink.

No such luck. The doorbell rang again and again, so many times Morrison lost count, and Karma groaned in frustration. "Damn, those Girl Guides! They have the *worst* timing ever."

"I'll be right back," he said, affectionately patting her hips. "Wait here. Don't move."

"Hurry back, or I'm starting without you!"

Chuckling, Morrison buttoned his shirt and fixed his crooked belt as he marched through the main floor. Sunshine poured through the skylights, and the floor-to-

ceiling windows throughout the estate provided striking views of the expansive grounds. A blend of modern
and rustic accents, with an open-concept living space,
Morrison loved that he could cook, drink wine, research
legal cases and watch ESPN on his big-screen TV all at
the same time.

In the foyer Morrison heard someone banging on the
front door, and peered through the peephole to see who
his visitor was. His mood soured faster than a cup of milk
left out in the sun. *What is Toya doing here? Doesn't she
have someone else to bother? Somewhere else to be?* In
the year she'd been dating his kid brother, he couldn't
recall her ever coming to his house alone, so Morrison
knew there was a problem. With Toya there always was.
She enjoyed drama, got off on arguing and debating with
people about hot-button issues, and Morrison didn't want
her at his house—not when he was about to sex Karma
on his kitchen counter.

Morrison gripped the door handle, turned it and
greeted his future sister-in-law with a warm smile, even
though he'd rather get a colonoscopy on live TV than
have a conversation with the petulant blonde. She was
there to discuss Roderick going to rehab, no doubt, but
Morrison played dumb, pretended he didn't know why
she was standing on his welcome mat.

"What a pleasant surprise," he lied, noting the peeved
expression on her face. Dressed in a striped crop top and
see-through leggings, her hair up in a messy ponytail,
he guessed Toya was on her way home from spin class,
and wished she'd driven past his house instead of dropping by unannounced. "What brings you to my neck of
the woods?"

"Who do you think you are?" Her hazel eyes narrowed and darkened with anger. "How dare you pres-

sure Roderick to go to rehab? He doesn't need treatment any more than you do, so get a life, and leave my man the hell alone."

Morrison spoke through clenched teeth. "Lower your voice. I have company."

"I don't care. I want this situation rectified today, before Roderick does something stupid and ruins our future." Her tone was shrill, panicked. "Tell him you've changed your mind about everything. Tell him he doesn't need to go to the Securities Exchange and Commission on Thursday or to rehab—"

"Sooner or later the SEC will uncover what Roderick did. They always do."

"Or not. For every guy they catch, ten go unnoticed, and Roderick will be one of the lucky ones." Toya put a hand on her chest. "I know it in my heart. Roderick's not going to jail. He did nothing wrong."

"It's obvious you're in denial, but Roderick is guilty of insider trading and he needs to do the right thing before it's too late." Lowering his head, Morrison pinched the bridge of his nose, tried his best to keep it together. He wasn't in the mood for Toya's nonsense. Wasn't going to give her the satisfaction of riling him up. "A real man takes responsibilities for his mistakes, Toya. He doesn't run from them."

"Do you hear yourself? You're talking crazy—"

"No, what's crazy is standing by and watching the man you say you love destroy himself with booze. Every day in this country healthy, young men like my brother die of alcohol poisoning and I'm not going to pretend he doesn't have a problem. Roderick needs help—"

"No, he doesn't. He's fine. Just because Roderick likes to unwind by having a couple drinks at the end of a long workday doesn't mean he has a problem. He doesn't. He's stressed out. That's all."

Morrison cringed. His estate was his sanctuary, his favorite place to relax and unwind, and Karma often joked it had more rooms than the Hyatt Hotel, but Toya was so loud Morrison knew Karma could hear what Toya was saying, and wished the spoiled and pampered princess would get the hell out. Morrison didn't argue with her, knew if he did, Toya would never leave, and he wanted her gone. Now. Before he lost his temper and said something he'd regret. Something that could ruin his close-knit relationship with his brother.

"You're going to fix this today," Toya announced.

"If you loved Roderick the way you say you do, you'd want what's best for him."

"You ass!" she cursed. "Of course, I want what's best for Roderick, but what I don't want is for us to be laughed at and gossiped about around town. Neither would your parents. What do you think will happen when they find out about your plans?"

Damn. Roderick still hadn't talked to their mom and dad? What was he waiting for? They didn't know about his meeting with the SEC next Thursday? The news was shocking, almost knocked Morrison off his feet. Toya's words gave him pause, made him realize he'd never considered how his parents would feel about Roderick's decision. Not because he didn't care, because he didn't feel it was his place to tell them. It wasn't too late to call a family meeting, and once Toya left he'd touch base with his brothers about it. "I don't mean to be rude, Toya, but I'm going to have to ask you to leave."

"I'm not going anywhere until you call Roderick and make this right."

As if it was her estate, and her name was on the deed,

Toya pushed past him and marched down the hallway and into the kitchen. Stopping abruptly, she glanced from Morrison to Karma, fine lines wrinkling her forehead. "Who are you?"

Smiling brightly, Karma waved and rose from her seat. "Hi. I'm Karma Sullivan."

"Toya Janssen. Are you one of Reagan's friends from Hampton Academy?"

"You think I'm a high school student?" Her face lit up. "Morrison, I like her *a lot.*"

Yeah, well, you're the only one. It was an open secret that his mom didn't like Toya, but for the sake of peace Viola kept her opinions to herself. Toya was living the high life and wanted Roderick to foot the bill, and that didn't sit well with his fiercely independent mother, and the other hardworking women in the Drake family.

Morrison stood beside Karma and put an arm around her waist. He was proud of her, loved showing her off and boasting about her accomplishments. He'd agreed to be her date for the Hamptons Women's Association banquet, and was convinced Karma would be named Businesswoman of the Year. "Karma's my girlfriend," he said, his chest puffed up with pride.

Toya's eyes bulged out of her head. "*You* have a girlfriend?"

"Yeah, and she's smart, successful and, as you can see, stunning."

"Did you meet at the courthouse? Karma, are you a judge too?"

"Me? A judge? No, I own the hottest new beauty salon in town, so the next time you need your hair, nails and makeup done come to Beauty by Karma, and I'll hook you up."

Leaving the women to talk, Morrison returned to the

stove to prepare the spinach-cranberry salad and par-
mesan garlic rolls. His mouth watered, and his stomach
groaned and growled at the aromas in the air.

"Morrison, this isn't over," Toya said, trailing behind
him. "Roderick has enough on his plate without you
stressing him out, so let him be."

Silently, Morrison counted to ten, told himself not to
argue with her, no matter what she said.

"Haven't you learned anything from Emmanuelle's
death? You're going to drive Roderick away, just like you
did your sister, and it could result in tragic consequences."

His stomach plunged to his feet.

"Toya, we'll discuss this another time—"

"No, we'll talk now," she insisted. "Karma needs to
know the kind of man she's dealing with, and I'm just
the person to tell her."

Her words were filled with such venom, Morrison
stared at her in disgust. Felt bad that his brother was mar-
rying a woman with no class. Toya had a pretty face and
a trim body, but she had a bad attitude. Still, he didn't
lash out at her. Morrison started to speak, but Karma interrupted him, surprised him by speaking up for herself,
and he appreciated her mature response.

"Toya, that's not necessary. Morrison is a great guy
who treats me exceptionally well, and there's nothing
you can say that will change the way I feel about him."

You tell her, baby! Morrison wanted to throw his hands
in the air and shout "Booyah!" in Toya's face, but since
he didn't want to make the situation worse he tamped
down his excitement and concentrated on chopping the
vegetables on the cutting board.

"We should do drinks sometime." Karma opened her
handbag, took out a business card and offered it to Toya.

"Give me a call. Maybe we can meet up one day next week."

"No, thanks. I have enough friends, and I don't need any more." Facing Morrison, she folded her arms rigidly across her chest. "Do you have to go to the SEC on Thursday? Can't you wait until after Roderick and I celebrate our anniversary on June twentieth? It's a big day for us, and I don't want to be alone."

"I thought Roderick was going to London for a week on business?"

"Yeah, but he'll, um, only be gone for a few days." The expression on her face softened. "Please, Morrison? I have something special planned for Roderick, and it would mean a lot to me if you could postpone the meeting."

Putting down the knife, Morrison considered Toya's request. Maybe he was wrong about her. Maybe she wasn't an opportunist who only cared about herself. Had he judged her too harshly? Toya was scared about the future, and Morrison didn't blame her. He was too. Couldn't stop thinking about the meeting with the SEC. Roderick's actions could have serious repercussions for his family, and in the back of his mind he was worried about his brother's choices affecting his Supreme Court aspirations. Filled with sympathy, he nodded his head. "I'll see what I can do."

Spinning around on her heels, Toya left without saying another word, mumbling under her breath about her life being over. Morrison wiped his hands on a dishcloth and followed her through the foyer. He wanted to see Toya get inside her Porsche and drive off before he locked the door and returned to the kitchen.

Reentering the room seconds later, Morrison dropped down on the couch. He needed a moment to gather himself. Karma sat beside him and rubbed his shoulder. She didn't speak, didn't have to. Just having her beside him was enough. Thinking about Emmanuelle always made him emotional, but he'd never felt closer to Karma, and wanted to confide in her about his sister. "Emmanuelle got into an argument with my parents one night during dinner about her horrible university grades, and when she disrespected my mom, I lost it. I told her she was a selfish, ungrateful brat who needed to grow up."

"Those are some harsh words."

"I lost my temper, and as soon as the words left my mouth I regretted them, but it was too late. Emmanuelle grabbed her purse, and stormed out of the mansion in a huff." Morrison swallowed hard. "That was the last time I saw her alive."

Moving closer to him, Karma hugged him tight, lovingly held him in her arms.

"For the life of me, I can't understand why my sister decided to go for a late-night swim after her best friend dozed off on the patio." Embarrassed that he couldn't control his emotions, Morrison stared down at the Persian rug so Karma couldn't see the tears in his eyes. "Emmanuelle loved the water and was an exceptional swimmer, so I don't know how she could have drowned. The coroner said she had a deadly mix of alcohol and prescription drugs in her system, and even after all these years none of it makes sense to me."

"Morrison, I am so sorry for your loss," Karma said in a quiet voice.

Overwhelmed by his emotions, he struggled to speak, couldn't get the words out. It never got easier talking about his sister's death, and he choked up every time he said her name. Morrison kept his head down, didn't want Karma to know he was hurting inside.

"Losing a loved one is the most helpless feeling in the world, and hard to cope with."

"I was in so much pain after Emmanuelle's death I thought I was going to die."

"That must have been a horrible time for you and your family."

"My sister's death brought us closer together, and I learned not to take the people I love for granted anymore," Morrison confessed. "Taking care of Reagan helped ease the pain, but not a day goes by that I don't miss Emmanuelle, or think about her. She will always carry a special place in my heart, and I will never forget her."

Karma nodded her head in understanding. "My mom and I were close, and my life feels empty without her. That's why I work nonstop. To fill the void, and distract me from the pain."

"You don't need to work eighty hours a week anymore. You have me."

"You're just as busy as I am," she countered. "Between work, meetings with your associates in Washington and keeping tabs on Reagan, you hardly have any free time, either."

Troubled by her words, Morrison felt the need to defend himself. "I know you think I'm hard on Reagan but at Emmanuelle's funeral I promised myself I'd do everything in my power to help my niece succeed. And I will."

"Success comes in many different forms, Morrison. I don't have an executive job in a fancy downtown office, or a lakefront mansion *yet*," she said with supreme confidence. "But I love what I do, and I'm a millionaire. I'm not keeping up with the Joneses. I *am* the Joneses!"

Eyes wide, his head snapped up. Morrison shouldn't have been surprised. Of course Beauty by Karma was doing well financially—Karma was the owner. She had more personality than a game show host and made friends wherever she went. "You're a millionaire? Wow, baby, that's great. The next time we go to SushiSamba for lunch you're picking up the check, so don't forget your platinum card!"

Karma giggled. "You wish! Speaking of lunch, where is it? I'm starving, so quit lounging around on the couch and get back to the kitchen."

"Typical New Yorker. You're not happy unless you're telling someone what to do," Morrison said with a laugh, helping Karma to her feet.

"What are you going to do about Toya?" she asked, a curious expression on her face.

"I'll reschedule our meeting with investigators at the SEC, but I'm not going to lie to Roderick to make Toya happy. He's my family, and I won't turn my back on him. He needs me now more than ever, and I have to help him."

"I admire your loyalty and commitment to your brother," Karma said, squeezing his hands. "Your family is lucky to have you watching over them."

"And I'm lucky to call you my girl."

Karma kissed his lips, slowly, tenderly, and a delicious sensation flooded his body. In that moment, Morrison realized he couldn't fight his feelings anymore. He wanted to be the only man in her life, for the rest of her life, and knew in his heart that Karma was the only woman for him. Cupping her face in his hands, he deepened the kiss, feasted on her lips.

"Let's start with dessert," she whispered against his mouth, her throaty, sultry voice betraying her need. "It's my favorite meal of the day."

Their eyes met, and Morrison knew they shared the same thought: *screw lunch!*

"Mmm. Something smells delicious in here."

"Hi, Uncle. Hi, Ms. Karma. What's good?"

"Mr. Drake, can we stay for lunch?"

Morrison cranked his head to the right, saw Reagan enter the kitchen with six of her friends from Hampton Academy and hung his head. *Damn. First Toya, and now this. I can't catch a break today!* Reagan turned the TV on to MTV, and hip-hop music filled the air.

"Looks like we have company," Karma said and dropped her hands from around his neck.

"I'll get rid of them."

"Don't be silly. I love hanging out with Reagan and her friends."

Morrison frowned. "Well, I don't, so let's go upstairs to my bedroom."

"Boy, stop. Now, be a good host and help me dish the food and get them drinks."

Springing into action, Karma grabbed plates from off the counter and served the group lunch, chatting with them about their exams, prom dresses and summer hairstyle trends.

Annoyed that his niece and her friends had ruined the mood, Morrison realized he wasn't getting dessert—or lunch—and strangled a groan.

Chapter 15

"I'm out of here. Bye, everyone!" Karma said with a smile, slinging her Gucci purse over one shoulder and her tote bag over the other. "Have a great night. See you tomorrow."

Breezing through the front door, Karma couldn't recall the last time she'd left Beauty by Karma at four o'clock, but Morrison and Reagan were on their way to pick her up for the Bruno Mars concert, and Karma wanted to toss her things in the trunk before they arrived. Thinking about Morrison and how much he meant to her made her heart smile. They'd only been dating for two months, but she'd already met his entire family, and next Sunday he was going with her to Brooklyn to have lunch with her grandparents. Karma had never brought anyone to their cozy brownstone before, and she hoped this would be the first of many visits. Last night, after making love, they talked about their relationship and their future, but Karma still couldn't bring herself to tell Morrison the truth about her past. He'd opened up to her about the death of his sister, and even though Karma felt even closer to him, she was scared of being vulnerable with him. He wouldn't understand. How could he? It was a scandalous, salacious story that Karma was taking to her grave.

Yawning, her eyes watered, blurring her vision. May had been the busiest, most lucrative month Beauty by Karma had ever had, and Karma was convinced Reagan and Eve, the loveable colorist, were the reason why they had more bookings than ever. Not only were the female students at Hampton Academy now visiting the salon, so were their relatives. And every time Karma pulled up to the salon, Eve was outside, handing out flyers and chatting with locals. She'd promoted Abigail from the receptionist position to salon manager a month ago, and what the single mom lacked in experience she more than made up for in personality. Quick to smile and laugh, she made clients feel welcome, and was eager to learn everything there was to know about the business.

Main Street was surprisingly quiet, deserted except for the brunettes snapping selfies in front of the gleaming, white sports car parked at the curb. Seeing the women hugging and laughing made Karma think of Jazz, and she wondered how her ex-friend was doing. If her social media pages were any indication, she was living the good life. Shopping at ritzy, by-appointment-only boutiques. Dining at premier restaurants. Flaunting the Cartier jewelry her boyfriend had given her. Boasting about their upcoming trip to Lake Como. Maybe one day, when the memory of their argument didn't hurt as much, they'd be friends again. That was Karma's hope. They'd had good times together, and despite their falling-out weeks earlier, she wanted the best for Jazz, hoped all of her dreams came true. And if Karma was wrong about Lorenzo, she'd be the first to apologize, but if she was right about the wealthy businessman, she'd ensure she was there to help her friend pick up the pieces.

"I've dreamed of us reuniting for months, actually the entire time I was incarcerated, but now that you're standing in front of me I don't know what to say."

Blinking, Karma surfaced from her thoughts, told herself she was imagining things, that the man with the grizzly voice wasn't her... Her legs buckled, and a gasp fell from her lips. Convinced something was wrong with her vision, Karma took off her sunglasses and narrowed her gaze, stared intently at the short, dark-skinned man standing in front of her. It was Feisal. She wasn't seeing things, wasn't sleeping with her eyes open, and assessed him from head to toe. He smelled like an ashtray, but his white, short-sleeve shirt and khaki pants were clean and ironed.

"Karma, honey, you look amazing," he praised, nodding his head. "It's obvious you've done well for yourself the last few years, and I'm proud of you."

Karma stepped back, wanted to get as far away from Feisal as possible. Nothing made sense. What was he doing here? Had he escaped from prison? Was he on the run? There was only one way to find out, so she coughed to clear the lump in the back of her throat and projected confidence, even though she was trembling all over.

"How did you find me? What are you doing here?" Karma glanced around to ensure no one was listening in on their conversation. "You're supposed to be in jail."

A frown curled his thin lips. "Didn't you get my letters? I was released from Livingston early for good behavior, and the first person I wanted to see was you."

"If you don't leave, I'll call the local police and have you arrested for harassment. I don't want you here. You're dead to me."

The light went out in his eyes, and his shoulders slumped. "Karma, I love you, and I miss you, and I want to have a relationship with you more than anything in the world. You have to believe me. You're all that matters to me."

His words blew her mind. Feisal was a liar who didn't have an honest bone in his body, and Karma didn't believe anything he said. It didn't matter that his eyes were filled with tears, didn't matter that he sounded sincere; he'd hurt her before, and given the chance he'd do it again. "Please leave—"

"I made a mistake, but I want to do right by you, and re-earn your trust."

"Are you out of your mind? You ruined my life, and I hate you!"

"You don't mean that, but I can see that you're upset so I'll come back another time."

"No! Don't!" she snapped, shouting her words. "Why is this so hard for you to understand? I don't want to see you again. *Ever.* Not tomorrow, not in a month, not in a year. Got it? You're not welcome here, and if I catch you anywhere near my shop I'll…"

Panic ballooned in her chest, drenching her skin with sweat, and Karma broke off speaking. Her body shook uncontrollably, and her stomach twisted in a knot. Morrison and Reagan were headed their way, walking straight toward her, and Karma feared what would happen if Morrison and Feisal came face-to-face. It felt like her legs weighed a thousand pounds each, but she stepped past Feisal and marched off, wanted to run full-speed down the street and into the comfort of Morrison's arms, but Karma maintained her composure.

"P-p-please don't do this," he pleaded, his voice filled with desperation. "I need you."

Deaf to his pleas, she blinked away the tears in her eyes and slapped a smile on her lips. Her temperature soared, and her pulse pounded, but since Karma didn't want Morrison to know she was upset, she spoke in a bubbly voice. "I thought you two would never get here," she joked, playfully wiggling her eyebrows. "We better get going, or we'll get stuck in traffic on our way to pick up Reagan's date. And I don't know about you guys but I don't want to miss even a second of the concert."

"Ms. Karma, what happened?" Reagan asked. "You're shaking."

Morrison gestured with his head behind her. "Did that man upset you?"

"No. I'm fine. Now, can we please go?"

Karma heard footsteps behind her, felt Morrison pull her to one side, and Reagan to the other, and even though she knew what was about to happen—her past colliding with her future—there was nothing she could do to stop it. Karma wanted to protect herself, to plead her case to Morrison, but when she opened her mouth the words didn't come.

"Sir, I think you should leave," Morrison said, shielding the women with his body. "You've upset my girlfriend, and I don't want us to have any problems."

Feisal raised an eyebrow. "You're Karma's boyfriend? But you're not her type."

Karma could feel the heat of Morrison's gaze, knew he was expecting her to say something, but her throat was dry, and it took every ounce of her strength to remain upright.

"Sir, I don't mean to be rude, but who are you?"

Feisal stuck out his right hand. "I'm Feisal Leonard. Karma's dad."

* * *

You're who? Morrison blinked rapidly, gave his head a shake to clear the cobwebs from his mind. Confused, he couldn't make sense of what the dark-skinned man had said, but when he looked at Karma, he knew in his gut that Feisal was telling the truth. The expression on her face was telling. Perspiration dotted her forehead, unshed tears filled her eyes, and she was fiddling with the cocktail ring on her left hand. "What the—"

Remembering his niece was standing behind him, listening in, he slammed his mouth shut, swallowing the curse on the tip of his tongue. "Reagan, wait for me in the car."

"We're still going to the concert, right?"

"Do as you're told," he snapped. "And go back to the BMW."

Karma spoke to Feisal in Spanish, but there was so much noise on the street, Morrison didn't hear what she said. Feisal turned and walked away, his head down, his shoulders hunched, and Morrison felt a rush of compassion. He wanted to know what Feisal's story was, had so many questions for Karma, he didn't know what to ask first. "Reagan, I need to talk to Karma alone."

"Fine," she said with a dismissive wave of her right hand. "I'll be in the salon. I need to use the bathroom, and I want to touch up my lipstick."

Out of the corner of his eye, he saw Reagan heading toward the shop, but waited until she was inside the salon before he spoke. "What was *that*?" he asked, pointing a finger in Feisal's direction. Morrison could see him in the distance, and wondered where he was going, and if he had any other family in the city besides his estranged daughter. "You told me your parents died in a car accident six years ago, and I believed you. Why would you make up such a horrific story? Is your mom alive too?"

"Morrison, I am so sorry. You weren't supposed to find out like this."

"Find out what? That the woman I love is a liar?"

Her eyes widened, and her lips parted wordlessly, but Morrison didn't let her off the hook, questioned her relentlessly about her father's unexpected arrival and her mother's whereabouts. The streets were noisy, filled with shoppers, men in designer suits talking business, teenagers goofing around in front of the ice cream shop, and early-evening traffic.

Karma glanced around nervously, and Morrison knew if they remained on the sidewalk she'd never answer his questions. Wanting privacy, he took her by the arm, led her over to his BMW and helped her inside. Memories flooded his mind as he got in beside her. The last time they'd been in the back seat of his SUV they'd ended up making love, and just thinking about the sensuous, erotic encounter days earlier made an erection rise inside his blue Levi's jeans.

"I deserve answers, Karma. I want to know why you lied to me about your family. Why you made up a story about your parents being dead when they're obviously not."

"I didn't lie. My mother died six years ago, and was laid to rest at Cypress Hills Cemetery, and as far as I'm concerned, so did my father. He's responsible for her death, and I hate him."

Taken aback by her harsh tone, he stared at her profile. She stared straight ahead, out the windshield, but he sensed her anger, the turmoil within. "*Hate*'s a strong word, Karma."

"It's an accurate word. Feisal's dead to me, and I don't want to see him ever again."

"Why? What did he do? Why are you estranged?"

Karma scoffed, wore a disgusted expression on her face. "You mean, besides the fact that he's been in the Livingston Correctional Facility for the past few years?"

Morrison rubbed his hands over his knees. He felt hot, claustrophobic in his own body, but he asked the question at the forefront of his mind. "Did you ever visit him in prison?"

"You're joking, right? No, never. Because of his poor choices, my mom is gone, and I don't know if I'll ever be able to forgive him." Sniffing, she dabbed at her eyes with her fingertips, then hugged her arms to her chest. "He took the person I love most away from me, and not a day goes by that I don't wake up, hoping her funeral was a bad dream…"

Morrison prided himself on being a good listener, but he struggled to concentrate on what Karma was saying because he couldn't stop thinking about Feisal. Couldn't forget the pained expression on his face, his slumped shoulders and hopeless demeanor as he'd walked away from them. Karma didn't have a mean bone in her body, and was open and honest about everything, so Morrison didn't understand why she'd deceived him about her past. Was Karma embarrassed because Feisal was an ex-con? Was she worried he'd reject her because her father had a criminal record? And, most important, what other secrets was Karma hiding?

"I opened up to you about Emmanuelle and even Roderick's personal struggles, and I wish you'd trusted me enough to confide in me about your family."

"Morrison, baby, of course I trust you. You're the best boyfriend I have ever had, and dating you has changed

me in so many ways. I never meant to deceive you. You
have to believe me." Facing him, Karma touched Morrison's hand and squeezed it. "You're a remarkable man,
Morrison, and I will never forget you."

A cold chill stabbed his flesh. Morrison had no words.
Couldn't think straight or move his lips. Her voice blared
in his ears, echoed in his heart, tormenting him. *You're
breaking up with me? After everything we've been
through? Don't you know how much I love you?* Floored
by her actions, Morrison didn't know what to say.

Silence filled the car, and tension hovered in the air
like smoke.

"Why are you doing this? Are you intentionally trying to hurt me?"

"No, of course not. You want to be a Supreme Court
judge, and only judges with a pristine job history, stellar
reputation and scandal- and corruption-free background
will be considered," she said, repeating what he'd told
her weeks earlier. "And if we continue dating, and the
powers that be find out about my background, you could
lose the thing you want more than anything, and I won't
let that happen."

Morrison straightened in his seat, tried his best to
conceal his frustration, the anger coursing through his
veins. "Don't I get a say in all this? Doesn't it matter
what *I* want?"

"You don't know what Feisal's like, or the horrible
things he's done in the past."

"Then tell me," he pleaded. "Because none of this
makes sense."

"The less you know about my family the better."

"You have different last names," Morrison pointed
out. "Is he your biological father?"

"After my mother died, I collected the money from the

life insurance policy and moved from Brooklyn to the Hamptons. For a fresh start, I took my mother's maiden name. Morrison, I'm sorry for not being honest with you about my past, but I was ashamed about it, and I was scared if I confided in you, you wouldn't want me."

Morrison dragged a hand down his face. Looking back, he realized he'd screwed up. Made a mistake. He'd been so smitten with Karma he'd failed to do his homework, and wished he'd taken the time to do a background check when they'd first started dating. Duane and Erikah had talked him out of it, said it was a sneaky thing to do, but now his heart was broken.

Karma leaned over and surprised him with a kiss. Her mouth was sweet, flavored with peppermint, and intoxicating. Karma had great hands, and just thinking about them on his body made his temperature rise. And when Karma pulled away disappointment consumed him.

"Goodbye, Morrison," she whispered against his mouth, gently stroking his face with her soft, warm hands. "Take good care of yourself, and Reagan."

"Karma, what are you doing? Where are you going? We have plans tonight."

"I don't want to do anything to derail your dreams, or ruin your future—"

"Please, don't do this. We can get through this."

Morrison flung open his door and jumped out of the car, desperate to reach her before it was too late. By the time he got on the sidewalk and spotted Karma, she was climbing inside her pink PT Cruiser. Shouting her name, Morrison knocked on the passenger-side window. He begged her to talk to him, but Karma sped off, leaving him alone on the busy street to figure out how he was going to live the rest of his life without the woman he loved more than anything.

Chapter 16

Morrison left the courthouse on Thursday afternoon feeling exhausted and spent after a long, grueling day behind the bench, and although he had plans to play golf with his brothers at the country club, he was going to cancel and go home. They'd understand. He hadn't been himself since Karma dumped him, and the past three days he'd thought of her and nothing else.

The sky was overcast, and gray, mirroring his bleak mood. Reading the day's headlines on his cell phone, Morrison deactivated his car alarm, tossed his briefcase in the back seat of his Lexus and slammed the door. He'd texted Karma yesterday, asking if they could meet up to talk, but she still hadn't responded to his message. Or the emails he'd sent that afternoon.

Happy memories filled his mind—kissing Karma for the first time, strolling through the botanical garden with her hand in hand, playing miniature golf and bowling—and a sad smile curled his lips. He'd never been shy about expressing his feelings to her, and now more than ever Morrison wanted Karma to know what was in his heart, didn't hold back in his messages. He admired her strength, how she'd beaten the odds and become a success, but what wowed him most about Karma was her inner beauty. Smart and effervescent, she was perfect for him in every way, and Morrison couldn't imagine his life without her.

"Morrison, I'd like to have a word with you."

Spotting Feisal standing near the trunk, Morrison wondered where he'd come from, and nodded his head in greeting. Short, with low-cropped, salt-and-pepper hair and a thin mustache, Morrison guessed he was in his late fifties. "What's on your mind?"

"Not here. Let's have a drink at a pub on Main Street."

"I'd prefer to go to the coffee shop around the corner," he said, putting on his sunglasses. "We can walk. I've been cooped up inside all day and could use some fresh air."

Heading south on Pantigo Road with Feisal, thoughts of Karma filled his mind—and questions he desperately needed answers to—but since he wanted to look Feisal in the eye when they spoke, Morrison decided to wait until they arrived at the café to ask him about his tumultuous relationship with his only daughter. They made small talk about the weather, sports and the Yankees' five-game losing streak.

Soft-spoken, but charismatic, Feisal had more stories than the six o'clock news, and Morrison was drawn to his easygoing personality. Like his daughter, he seemed genuine and sincere, and spoke in glowing terms about his late wife and her close-knit family.

Entering the café ten minutes after leaving the court-house, Morrison noticed the simple, but tastefully deco-rated shop was empty and sat down at a round table. The café offered baked goods, sandwiches and hot beverages. The scent of cinnamon and freshly brewed coffee sweet-ened the air. Morrison was still full from lunch, but he encouraged Feisal to order something, and handed him one of the white, laminated menus.

"Five dollars for a cup of coffee? Eight bucks for a bowl of clam chowder? Twelve bucks for a double cheeseburger and sweet potato fries?" Feisal whistled, an awestruck expression on his wide face. "I'll eat back at the motel. I'm hungry, but these prices are a little too steep for my blood. I'm a regular guy, not a Rockefeller."

Morrison took his wallet out of his back pocket, opened it and put a fifty dollar bill on the table. "Feisal, it's on me. Get whatever you want."

"In that case, I'll have all three, and a side of potato salad."

The waiter took his order, jotted it down on a notepad, then marched into the kitchen.

"Thanks, son, I appreciate it. Money's real tight for me right now, and if not for my uncle Clive lending me a few bucks and his old Buick I never would have made it out here."

"Mr. Leonard, where are you staying?"

"Do me a favor, would ya? Call me Feisal. Sounds cooler, don't you think?" Wearing a wry smile, he cracked his knuckles, then clasped his hands on the table. "I'm staying at the Hamlet Inn. It's nothing fancy, but it's a hell of a lot better than Livingston Correctional Facility, and the owners are pleasant."

"I'm glad you came by the courthouse," Morrison confessed. "I wanted us to talk before you returned to the city—"

"What makes you think I'm leaving? I came here to reunite with my daughter, and I'm not going a damn place until we reconcile. Karma's all I've got left, and I won't lose her."

The waiter returned, emptied her tray onto the table and gave a polite nod.

"Feisal, what happened? Why does Karma hate you?"

His spoon fell from his hand, struck his soup bowl and dropped to the floor.

"You don't know?" he asked, his eyes the size of golf balls. "She never told you?"

"No, we haven't been dating long, and before Thursday I didn't even know you existed." Morrison felt his cell phone buzz from inside the pocket of his charcoal-gray suit pants, but decided to let the call go to voice mail. He'd didn't want to miss a word Feisal said, and hoped he'd help him make sense of the emotional conversation he'd had with Karma days earlier. To put Feisal at ease, Morrison told him about the first time he met Karma, her birthday weekend, their fishing excursions and her incredible relationship with his niece. "Did I say something wrong?" Morrison asked, noticing the frown on Feisal's face.

"My daughter must be sweet on you..."

God, I hope so. I love her with all my heart and I want her to be my wife.

"Because she hates fishing. Always has. Says it's a boring waste of time—"

"Why does Karma blame you for her mother's death?" Morrison blurted out, anxious to hear the truth.

With zero hesitation, he said, "Because I was a poor excuse for a husband and an absentee father during Karma's teens. I loved my wife and daughter, but my inability to provide for them after an accident at work left me with chronic back pain, made me feel ashamed and inadequate, and over time I pulled away from them."

Morrison straightened in his chair, listened with rapt attention as Feisal discussed his addiction to prescription drugs and his decades-old gambling habit. Owing thousands of dollars to a Brooklyn crime boss, with no means to pay, he'd stopped hanging out with his friends at the local bars and kept a low profile. He'd had a chip on his shoulder, and more enemies than friends, but he'd never dreamed the bad choices he'd made would cost him his family.

"One night, as my wife and I were leaving to have dinner at her favorite Creole restaurant, two masked men shot at my Subaru," Feisal explained, tears filling his deep brown eyes. "I was shot twice in the leg, a-a-and… Carmelita was pronounced dead at the scene."

Pushing away his plate, he dropped his face in his hands, and blew out a deep breath.

"The cops found an unregistered gun in the glove compartment of my car and arrested me on the spot. I was charged and sentenced to five years in jail for the offense. You're a judge, so I know you think I'm a loser, but I'm not."

"No, I don't. Everyone makes mistake and deserves a second chance."

Feisal wiped at his tear-stained cheeks. "Do you really mean that?"

"I lost my kid sister ten years ago, but I still regret the horrible things I said to her when we argued during a family dinner." Morrison picked up his glass and guzzled down the ice-cold water, hoped it cooled his sweltering body temperature. "I didn't know that was the last time I'd see Emmanuelle alive. If I did, I would have hugged her, instead of insulting her."

Feisal wore a sympathetic expression on his face and nodded in understanding.

"I've made a lot of mistakes in my life, and screwed

up more times than I can count, but I loved my wife and daughter more than anything. I always will."

His heart was full of compassion, and even though Morrison had just met Feisal, his gut was telling him that Karma's dad was being sincere, speaking the truth. "I'm going to help you."

"With what?"

For the first time since they'd arrived at the café, Morrison smiled. "Reuniting with your daughter, of course. Don't worry, Feisal. I've got this. Leave everything to me."

"Th-th-thanks, man. I don't know how I'll ever repay you," he stammered in a raspy voice. Tears filled his eyes and spilled down his cheeks, splashing onto his plaid, short-sleeve shirt. "I'll be right back. I need to use the men's room."

Staring out the window, Morrison's gaze fell across the woman with the dyed purple hair in front of the coffee shop, and his thoughts turned to Karma. He couldn't accept that she didn't want to date him. Morrison hadn't told anyone about their breakup, and didn't plan to. The only thing he knew for sure was that he wasn't letting Karma go. Not without a fight.

Morrison's cell rang, and he took it out of his pocket. He had six missed calls, and they were all from Roderick. Morrison wondered if his brother was having second thoughts about their meeting with the SEC tomorrow morning, and wanted him to know he had his back. Pressing the answer button, he put his cell to his ear, anxious to touch base with his kid brother about his business trip. "Roderick, what's up?" he said, trying to sound upbeat, even though he was miserable inside. Life wasn't the same without Karma, wasn't as exciting or fun, and every day without her was unbearable. But for this brother's sake, he pretended life was good. "How was London? Were you able to successfully renegotiate the deal with European Records for your client, or is their legal team still reviewing the third draft of the contracts?"

"She cleaned me out! Took everything in the house that wasn't nailed down," Roderick shouted. "Can you believe this shit? She played me for a fool, and I never saw it coming."

Wincing, Morrison moved his cell away from his ear. "Roderick, slow down. You're not making any sense. What's going on?"

"Aren't you listening?" he snapped. "Toya's gone, and she took everything I own."

Morrison nodded, though his brother couldn't see him, and rose to his feet. Nothing mattered more to him than being there for Roderick, so he gestured to the waiter for the check and hoped Feisal returned soon from the men's room.

Taking his car keys out of his pocket, he made a mental note to text Duane once he got off the phone. He'd know what to do. Morrison wasn't himself right now, was still troubled about his breakup with, Karma, and needed Duane's quiet wisdom to help calm Roderick down. "Bro, hang tight. I'll be there in twenty minutes."

"Don't bother. My place looks pitiful, and I don't want you to see it like this…"

Roderick's voice broke, and he trailed off speaking. *Damn. Is he crying?*

"Bro, I don't care about your house. I care about you."

"I need my space. No offense, Mo, but I want to be alone right now."

Morrison scoffed, shook his head in disbelief as he listened to his brother explain why he couldn't come to his Southampton estate. His mind made up, Morrison pretended he didn't hear what Roderick said, and spoke in a stern tone. "Don't move, Roderick. I'm on my way."

Morrison entered Roderick's sprawling, twelve-bedroom estate, noticed there was no furniture any-where on the main floor and swallowed hard. The air smelled of herbs and tobacco, and footsteps pounded on the marble floors, echoing throughout the estate. He found his brothers in the living room. Duane was lean-ing against the bare, powder blue walls, typing on his cell phone, and Roderick paced the length of the room, puffing on a cigar.

"I'm glad you're here," Duane said in a quiet voice, pocketing his cell phone. "Roderick is trippin' big-time, and I don't blame him. Toya did him dirty."

"Really? I thought maybe he was exaggerating. You know how he gets sometimes."

"It's bad. She took the furniture, the silverware, the bedding and even the toilet paper."

Roderick glanced in their direction, and Morrison's heart filled with sympathy.

"I'd offer you a seat, bro, but as you can see I don't have any."

"Don't sweat it, Roderick." Morrison didn't know what to say, didn't know how to comfort his brother, and said the first thing that came to mind. "How are you hold-ing up?"

"I told you, Toya screwed me over. Isn't this some messed-up reality-TV-type shit?"

Morrison gulped. Remembering his last conversation with Toya, heat burned his cheeks, and his shoulders slumped. "Toya tricked me. She said she was planning a surprise for your anniversary, and asked me for a favor.

That's why I postponed our meeting with the SEC. So that you guys could celebrate in style."

"She lied to you. Our one-year anniversary was last month, and we celebrated with a romantic dinner at her favorite Greek restaurant and a helicopter ride." Hanging his head, Roderick raked a hand through his hair. "Damn, Toya really played you. She asked you to postpone the meeting, so she could move out while I was in London."

Riddled with guilt, Morrison wished the ground would open and swallow him up. "Bro, I'm sorry. I had no idea what she was up to. If I'd known, I would have warned you."

"Apparently, no one knew. I've called all of her friends, and no one's seen her." Roderick cracked his knuckles. "Toya must have hired a removal team, because there's no way she carried out the furniture and artwork with her girlfriends."

"Damn, bro, I'm sorry. I can only imagine how you feel."

"Like a jackass who got screwed. I knew Toya was upset about me going to rehab, and my meeting with the SEC but I never dreamed she'd do something like this. Our wedding is in three months. What will people think?"

The brothers fell silent.

"It's not all bad," Duane said, glancing around at the barren space. "Now you can decorate your place the way you want, and we're going to help you."

Morrison agreed. "Yeah, we'll get some fresh, new paint, some designer furniture and sports memorabilia, and make this mansion the bachelor pad of your dreams."

"You know what the worst part is? She emptied our joint bank accounts." Roderick dragged a hand down the length of his face. "The money to repay the SEC is gone. All of it."

Morrison and Duane shared a look, and Roderick took a puff of his Cuban cigar.

"I'm going to find her and get my stuff back. And every damn penny she stole," he fumed, balling his hands into fists. "I need to know why Toya did this, why she betrayed me."

"Isn't it obvious?" Morrison said with a sympathetic expression on his face. "She's selfish, and self-absorbed, and only cares about herself. Forget her, bro. You don't need her."

"I know you're upset about what Toya did, but we're meeting with the SEC tomorrow, and I need you to be focused. We can't blow this."

"And, as for the money, don't worry about it," Morrison said. "We've got you."

Roderick stopped pacing. "You do?"

"Of course we do. We're your brothers."

"Really?" His eyes widened. "But I have to repay over a million dollars."

"It wouldn't matter if you owed ten million," Duane said, ruffling his brother's short hair. "We love you, and we're going to help you. That's what family does."

To make his brothers laugh, and lighten the mood, Morrison cracked a joke. "This is a one-time loan, bro. If you get in trouble with the SEC again you're on your own. *And*, I'll kick your ass up and down East Lake Drive!"

Chuckling, Roderick wiped his face with the bottom of his T-shirt. "Thanks, guys."

"Don't sweat it. What are brothers for?" Morrison said, lobbing an arm around his brother's hunched shoulders. "Love you, bro, and don't you forget it!"

"Mom's going to have a field day setting you up, you

know that, right?" Duane wiggled his eyebrows, made a silly face. "Viola's the original millionaire matchmaker, and once she finds out you're on the market, there'll be no stopping her."

Roderick groaned, as if he had indigestion, and shook his head. "Naw, bro, I'm through with the opposite sex. Done. I'm flying solo from here on out."

Duane scoffed, and Morrison wore a skeptical expression on his face.

"I'm serious, you guys." Bitterness filled his voice and darkened his eyes. "Women like Erikah and Karma are rare, and I hope you two knuckleheads know how fortunate you are to have smart, successful females in your corner who love you unconditionally, and have your best interests in heart. Not everyone is so lucky."

In that moment, Morrison, realized what was at stake, what would happen if he didn't show Karma how much he loved her. That she was the only one for him. That he couldn't live without her. A plan formed in his mind, and a grin claimed his mouth. Morrison knew what he had to do. He was getting his girl back, and nothing was going to stand in his way. To pull it off, he'd need his friends and family in on his plan, every last one of them. Morrison was getting Karma back and nothing was going to stand in his way.

Chapter 17

"Ms. Karma, you came!" Reagan shot across the backyard of the tree-lined estate and threw her arms around Karma's neck. "I wasn't sure if you were coming, so I'm stoked to see you!"

"I didn't have much of a choice. Erikah got her hair done at the salon this morning and threatened to key my car if I didn't come to your graduation party, so here I am," Karma joked with a laugh. "Just kidding. This is a momentous milestone for you, and I wouldn't miss it for anything in the world."

Her face lit up. "Were you at the ceremony? Did you hear my valedictorian speech? Did you see me walk the stage in my snazzy cap and gown?"

"Yes, yes, and yes." Karma gave the teen a hug. "You looked poised on stage, sounded wise beyond your years, and I'm proud of you. I screamed and cheered so loud during your speech that my throat is hoarse now!"

All across the backyard, Reagan's friends and family ate, talked and danced. The DJ was playing popular music, the waitstaff ensured champagne flutes were full of sparkling apple cider, and the photographer captured every memorable moment on his high-powered digital camera.

Cheers and boisterous laughter filled the air, drawing Karma's gaze to the teenage boys playing cornhole toss with graduation-themed bags. The caterer had done an outstanding job incorporating all of Reagan's favorite things, and the popcorn bar, candy station and advice tree—where friends and family could leave notes, good wishes and advice—was a hit among guests. Photo wreaths, filled with childhood pictures of Reagan, decorated the backyard, gold helium balloons were tied to evergreen trees, and the confetti cake was shaped to look like a graduation cap.

Karma reached into her purse and took out the red, heart-shaped envelope. "Here, sweetie, this is for you. Don't spend it all in one place."

Reagan squealed. Plucking the card out of Karma's hand, she danced to the beat of the music, waved her arms wildly in the air. "Thanks, Ms. Karma! You're the best."

"It's my pleasure. You've been a model student and an exceptional employee, so buy yourself something special." Karma wore a sad smile. "I'm going to miss you when you go off to school in the fall, but you're destined for great things so knock 'em dead!"

The light in her eyes dimmed and sadness flickered across her face. "I changed my mind. I'm going to live at home, instead of on campus, and I won't be going to beauty school."

"Why not? You were excited about leaving town, and you cried tears of joy when you received your acceptance letter to the Aveda Institute. What happened to change your mind?"

"I know, but if I go to beauty school I'd have to live in

the city, and Uncle Morrison is dead set against me living in a dorm or getting my own apartment."

"And, how do you feel about that?" Karma asked.

"At first I was upset, but my uncles made me realize how much Uncle Morrison has sacrificed for me, and I don't want to upset him. I want to make him proud, and I will."

Saddened by the teen's confession, Karma took her hand and squeezed it. It bothered her that Reagan was giving up her dreams to please her family, and Karma would never forgive herself if she didn't say something to Morrison. She searched the backyard for him, but couldn't find him anywhere, suspected he was inside the kitchen instructing the waitstaff. It had been seven days since they'd argued in front of her salon—a long, miserable week—and although she'd convinced herself that their breakup was for the best, Karma wanted to see him again, longed to kiss him, and touch him and hold him in her arms—

"Thanks again for coming, Ms. Karma. It means a lot to me…"

Blinking, Karma surfaced from her thoughts, pushed all images of Morrison from her mind. Forced herself to concentrate on what Reagan was saying instead of searching the grounds for Morrison. Where was he? Was he inside with one of the pretty single moms? Flirting, talking and laughing in an intimate corner, far away from the crowd?

"I know you're probably sick of hearing me say this, but I think you and Uncle Morrison make a great couple," Reagan said, gripping Karma's shoulders. "I know he can be stubborn sometimes, but don't give up on him. He's a good guy."

All Karma could do was nod her head. She didn't have

the heart to tell Reagan that she wasn't Morrison's girl-friend anymore, still hadn't come to terms with the news herself, but made a mental note to speak to Reagan in pri-vate when she arrived at the salon on Friday for her shift.

"I *love* this song," Reagan gushed, snapping her fin-gers. Looking pretty and youthful in a turquoise dress, her short, auburn curls bouncing around her face as she swayed to the music. "This is my jam. Let's dance, Ms. Karma."

"You go ahead. I'll see you later." Karma nudged Rea-gan toward her friends, who were partying under the oversize tent. "Have fun. It's your graduation party, so cut loose."

"I will. You can bet on it!" Giggling, the teen waved as she rushed off.

Thirsty, Karma walked across the lawn toward the dessert table. Mrs. Drake wore a polite smile, Mr. Drake raised his champagne flute in her direction and Duane waved. She wanted to breeze past them, was worried if she stopped to talk they'd question her incessantly about Feisal, but before Karma could decide what to do either way, Mrs. Drake slid in front of her, blocking her path. Her temperature soared, but she wore a bright smile.

"Karma, dear, how lovely to see you again." Mrs. Drake kissed her on both cheeks. Tall and slender, with a regal air, she had a warm and friendly demeanor. "I'm going to Marseille at the end of the month to do some shopping, and I want you and Erikah to join me, so clear your schedule, pack light and brush up on your French."

What French? I don't know any! Karma didn't know what to say. Couldn't get a word out. Stared at Mrs. Drake with wide eyes. Why didn't Morrison tell his parents the truth? What was he waiting for? She'd expected things to be awkward between them when she'd arrived at the graduation ceremony that afternoon, but thankfully it wasn't. Morrison was his usual charming, charismatic self, and sitting beside him in the auditorium, whispering and laughing, reminded Karma of all the good times they'd had. If not for Feisal, they'd still be dating, but now that her secret was out she had no choice but to distance herself from the man she loved—

"I want my sons and their wives to be one, big happy family so the more time we spend together the better." Mrs. Drake shielded her mouth with one hand and clutched her pearl necklace with the other. "I still can't believe what that girl did to my baby. I hope for Toya's sake I never cross paths with her again, because if I do I'll beat her with my Gucci handbag!"

A giggle tickled Karma's throat, but she didn't laugh. Knew if she did she wouldn't be able to stop. That morning, Erikah had spilled the tea about Roderick and Toya's breakup and Karma still couldn't believe what she'd heard. Though she hadn't spent much time with the couple, they'd seemed to really love each other, and every time she saw Roderick, he praised his fiancée. Wondering how the entertainment attorney was holding up, Karma searched for him among the well-dressed guests, but didn't find him.

"What are you two over here whispering about?" Joining them, holding her youngest child in her arms, Erikah blew her bangs out of her eyes. The mother of four was a respected pediatrician with a thriving medical practice, and one of the funniest people Karma had ever met. They'd instantly hit it off and enjoyed spending time together. "Tell me."

"That hazel-eyed hussy!" Mrs. Drake said, speaking through clenched teeth. "I'm so angry about what she did to Roderick, I could spit."

Erikah gasped, but Karma could tell by the amused expression on her round, plump face that she was trying hard not to laugh at her mother-in-law. Out of the corner of her eye, she spotted Morrison and Reagan posing for a picture under the graduation banner and smiled to herself. They looked cute together, like a doting father with his beloved daughter, and the image warmed her heart. Made her reflect on her relationship with her dad. She hadn't seen or heard from Feisal since he'd showed up unannounced at her shop and, for some strange reason, Karma wondered how he was doing.

Caught up in her thoughts, Karma didn't notice Morrison was standing in front of her until he slid an arm around her waist and whispered in her ear, "Looking for me?"

Electricity flooded her body, and the baby-fine hairs on the back of her neck shot up.

"Morrison, hey, what's up? How's it going?" Her voice sounded squeaky, foreign to her ears, but she wore a confident smile, didn't want Morrison to think she was weak for him, even though her palms were sweaty, and her pulse was racing out of control. Clasping her hands, Morrison led her away from his family to a quiet corner of the backyard.

"You look incredible," he praised, an appreciative smile on his lips. "I love your dress."

"Of course you do. You bought it for me when we went shopping at Chic Boutique."

Morrison snapped his fingers. "That's right. I did. Man, I have great taste in clothes!"

"*Someone's* ego is out of control," she quipped with a laugh.

"And it should be. I'm dating the most captivating woman in the Hamptons."

Her mouth fell open. *You are?*

"I'm going to start calling you Extra, because it's the perfect nickname for you."

"Extra?" Karma repeated. "Why?"

"Because you're extraordinarily smart, extraordinarily talented and extraordinarily beautiful. Best of all, you're mine, and I plan to cherish you as long as we both shall live."

Water filled her eyes, but Karma smiled through her tears. She was so moved by his words that she leaned over and kissed his lips. His mouth was warm, flavored with wine, the best thing she had ever tasted. "Morrison, thank you," she said, slowly caressing his face. "That's the sweetest thing anyone's ever said to me."

"Baby, I need to have you. Now. I've missed you so much."

Karma glanced around the backyard. Guests were too busy eating and dancing to pay them any mind, but she feared what would happen if someone came looking for them, and caught them in the act—Toya wouldn't be the only person on Mrs. Drake's hit list. Unwilling to take the risk, Karma shook her head. "Morrison, we can't—"

"*Can't* isn't in my vocabulary, and it shouldn't be in yours either."

Her body yearned to make love to him, to erase the pain of their argument, but Karma resisted the needs of her flesh. "Not now, Morrison, later. After the party ends."

"Fine, you win, but I need your help with Reagan's gift, so follow me inside."

"You bought her a hoverboard?"

"So she can break her neck and every other bone in her body? Heck no!" Morrison chuckled, laughed as if her question was the funniest thing he'd ever heard. "I bought her the six-piece Louis Vuitton luggage set, and I know she's going to love it."

"That's cool too."

"Damn right it is, and expensive too. It cost more than her Mini Cooper!"

"Speaking of Reagan, she told me you're dead set against her going to beauty school part-time and living on campus," she said, recalling the conversation she'd had earlier with the teen. "Morrison, I know you're worried something bad will happen to her, but you can't protect Reagan forever. You have to let her fall, so she can get back up and learn from her mistakes. Trust that you raised her right, and she'll make good choices, whether or not you're around."

"You sound like Roderick and Duane. They think I'm controlling, but I'm not."

"You most certainly are!" Karma quipped, fervently nodding her head to emphasize her point. "You make helicopter moms look sane."

Morrison scoffed. "You're exaggerating. I'm not that bad, am I?"

Wearing a sly smile, she reached out and patted his cheek. "No, baby, you're worse."

He chuckled, laughed out loud, but Karma could tell by the expression on his face that she'd given him something to think about.

"Maybe you're right," Morrison said with a shrug, shoving his hands into his pockets. "I've been doing some soul searching the past few days, and realized I need to advise less, listen more and let Reagan decide what's best for her."

To make him laugh, Karma snapped her fingers and swiveled her neck. "Of course I'm right. I'm *always* right. And don't you forget it."

Taking her in his arms, he held her close to his chest. "Thanks for supporting Reagan, and for encouraging her to follow her dreams."

Karma beamed when he caressed her back and kissed her forehead. *God, I love when he does that.* A quintessential gentleman with a big heart, he opened doors for her, pulled out chairs, spoiled and pampered her whenever they were together, and treated her with such warmth and tenderness Karma knew no one else could ever take his place in her heart. Karma loved the idea of settling down with Morrison, pictured their wedding day over and over again in her mind, but tempered her excitement. Even if they got back together, they still had several challenges to overcome. What if Feisal sold his story to the local newspaper to embarrass her? What would Mr. and Mrs. Drake think when they discovered her father was an ex-con? Would they threaten to disown Morrison if he continued dating her?

Morrison led her across the backyard, and through the wide open French doors. Inside, family members relaxed in the living room, servers moved around the kitchen, filling champagne flutes and appetizer trays, and Morrison's father and uncles played dominoes at the dining room table, arguing and shouting about every point. Karma followed Morrison through the main floor, past the spiral staircase in the foyer and into his corner office.

Spotting the luggage set in front of the floor-to-ceiling windows, the handles adorned with bows and ribbons, Karma said, "They're gorgeous. Good job, Morrison. And you're right. Reagan's going to love it, especially the vintage trunk. It looks chic and expensive."

"Hello, Karma. It's great to see you again."

Spinning around on her heels, she noticed Feisal standing in the opposite corner of the room, and dropped Morrison's hand. "Wh-wh-what's going on?" she stammered. "What is he doing here?"

"I invited him. He met Duane at the sports complex a couple days ago when we played tennis, but I want to introduce him to the rest of my family."

"No! Why? He doesn't deserve your kindness."

"I disagree. Feisal's humble, he's got a great sense of humor and he tells the best stories. I especially like the ones about his wisecracking daughter who used to be obsessed with Ja Rule, velour tracksuits and her Nokia flip phone." Morrison gripped Karma's arms, stared down at her with a sympathetic expression on his face. "Baby, hear him out."

"If you knew what he did you wouldn't be pressuring me to speak to him."

"Karma, he knows," Feisal said in a strong voice, stepping out of the shadows. "We had coffee together last week and I told Morrison about my past run-ins with the law and the circumstances surrounding your mother's death. He listened and didn't judge me, and I'm grateful."

Your mother's death…death…death… Karma pressed her eyes shut, willed the tears not to fall. His words echoed through her brain, piercing her heart, and she dropped her gaze to the plush carpet. Ice spread through her veins, chilling her to the bone, and the weight of Karma's grief was so heavy she couldn't lift her head.

"Do you know what kills me inside? What I regret more than anything? That I never had the opportunity to apologize to Emmanuelle for the horrible things I said to her that fateful night…" His voice cracked, and seconds passed before he spoke. "I should have talked to her privately, instead of going off on her. If I had, my sister might still be alive today."

"And if I had been the husband and father my wife

needed me to be, she'd be here with us celebrating."
Clearing his throat, Feisal tugged at the collar of his
black, V-neck shirt. "Karma, there hasn't been a day in
my life that I haven't thought about Carmelita, or what
I would have done differently. I am sorry for not being
the father I should have been, but I'm here now, and if
you can find it in your heart to forgive me I'd be most
grateful."

"I don't know if I can," she blurted out, hugging her
arms to her chest to stop her body from shaking. "I've
been angry at you for so long I don't know if I can ever
get past it."

"I understand. It's going to take time. I don't expect
things to change overnight." Feisal stepped forward. "I'll
have to work hard to gain your trust, and I will."

He sounded wounded, broken up inside, and the pain
in his voice touched her soul.

"I love you, honey. You have to believe me."

Karma didn't realize she was crying until Feisal
reached out and wiped her cheeks with his fingertips.
She saw the anguish in his eyes, the sadness, and realized
he was still grieving too. A quiet calm descended over
her, and Karma knew she was doing the right thing—
what her mom would want her to do—and embraced her
father for the first time in years.

Chapter 18

Karma sat at her office desk, proofreading the business plan she was to submit to the loan officer at Bridgehampton National Bank first thing tomorrow morning, but her thoughts were a million miles away. Between work, going on dates with Morrison and helping Reagan decorate her campus dorm room, she hadn't had much time to spend on the proposal, but Erikah said it was well written, and Karma was confident she'd secure a loan for her expansion project.

Drumming her fingers on her desk, Karma considered her schedule. July had been an insanely busy month, filled with dozens of consultations, out-of-town jobs, social events and dates with Morrison. They'd enjoyed dining five-star restaurants, Broadway musicals, stargazing at their favorite park and dancing at Manhattan nightclubs. Every Sunday, they'd visited her grandparents in Brooklyn, and it was the highlight of Karma's week. They'd eat a large, home-cooked meal, listen to Motown records on her grandfather's vintage turntable and play bid whist for hours at the dining room table.

Her gaze strayed from the computer monitor to the

picture frame beside the pink, reading lamp. The photograph had been taken at the Hamptons Women's Association banquet, and every time Karma looked at the image her heart smiled. When Morrison bragged to his family that she'd been nominated for the Businesswoman of the Year award, his parents and siblings had insisted on attending the event. Though she didn't win the award, she'd had fun at the banquet with the Drake family, her staff and her father. In the dimly lit ballroom, they talked, toasted and danced the night away. There was no better feeling than being in Morrison's arms, and just when Karma thought she couldn't love him anymore, he'd surprised her with two tickets to see the musical *Hamilton* to celebrate their four-month anniversary.

Touching the glass with her fingers, Karma marveled at how much her life had changed since meeting Morrison. Not only had his parents, siblings and nephews welcomed her into their family with open arms, they'd accepted her father, as well. Still struggling from the effects of his hip replacement surgery, and needing help around the estate, Nathaniel had hired Feisal to be his assistant, and gave him a room in the guesthouse. Feisal was flourishing in his new role, easily making friends around town and mentoring troubled youth in his old neighborhood on his days off, and Karma was proud of her dad for turning his life around. Thanks to Erikah, she'd found a family counselor, and twice a week, Karma and Feisal met with the affable, soft-spoken therapist. It could take months, even years, before they had a healthy father-daughter relationship, but Karma was glad she'd listened to Erikah about seeking professional help, and was learning a lot about her father during the hour-long sessions.

Thoughts of her mother filled her mind, and tears

pricked the back of her eyes. If Carmelita was alive, she'd be celebrating her fifty-sixth birthday. To mark the occasion, she'd taken fifty-six red roses to the cemetery that morning, and spent hours "talking" to her mom about her career, her relationship with Morrison and his family, and reuniting with her dad. It was an emotional visit that left Karma feeling drained, and she was thankful she'd taken Feisal up on his offer to drive her to Brooklyn.

"Do you have a minute to visit with an old friend?"

Karma blinked, spotted Jazz standing in the doorway and leaped to her feet. Her arms outstretched, she crossed the room and greeted her friend with a hug. They hadn't seen or spoken to each other since Jazz quit, and Karma was thrilled about the unexpected visit.

"Of course I have time for you. It's great to see you, Jazz," she said, meaning every word. Giving her the once-over, she admired her bold, cutout dress and her new hairdo. The sleek, two-toned bob framed her face perfectly, accentuated her cheekbones and gave her a fun, youthful vibe. "How have you been?"

"Great, but I *really* miss you."

"I miss you too. We had some incredible times here at the salon, and I cherish those memories," Karma confessed with a sad smile. "How are things going with Lorenzo?"

"Better than ever. He filed for divorce last month."

Shock must have registered on her face, because Jazz raised a hand in the air, as if swearing an oath in court, and fervently shook her head.

"Lorenzo and his estranged wife had problems long before I came along, and were legally separated when I met him at the gym," she explained. "I regret putting you in the middle of my relationship drama though. That wasn't cool, and I'm sorry."

"Apology accepted." Raising an eyebrow, Karma gave her friend the once-over. "Lorenzo must be a good guy. You're glowing!"

"We're renting a mansion in East Hampton, and having a lot of fun together. He's the most incredible man I've ever met, and I've never been happier."

I know just how you feel, Karma thought, unable to wipe the goofy, lopsided smile off her face either. *I'm madly in love with Morrison, and I want to spend the rest of my life with him.*

"I'm sorry about the things I said about Lorenzo, and for cramming my opinions down your throat," she said in a quiet voice. "I had no right to judge him, and I'm glad I was wrong about him."

"I got so caught up in Lorenzo, and our red-hot romance, I stopped being a good employee and friend, and I'm ashamed of how I treated you." Jazz hung her head. "I know I've been a pain in the ass, but I hope you can find it in your heart to forgive me. You're not just a friend, you're my family, and all I want is my bestie back."

"I do too." Karma gave Jazz another hug, rocked her vigorously from side-to-side to make her laugh, and kissed her cheek. Just yesterday, she'd been telling Morrison how much she missed Jazz, and here she was... Karma frowned. Had Morrison reached out to Jazz? Had he convinced her to come to the salon? Was he behind her friend's unexpected visit? Curious, she opened her mouth to ask the questions running through her mind, but Jazz interrupted her, and Karma lost her train of thought. It didn't matter. Her bestie was back at the salon, talking and laughing with her, and that was all that mattered.

"Let's have drinks at Oreya Restaurant and Lounge," Jazz proposed, tucking her purse under her arm. "It's my treat. I want to hear all about you and Morrison, the

Hamptons Women's Association banquet and your fabulous new clients, of course."

"I can't tonight, but tomorrow I'm all yours. It's Morrison's birthday, and I have a special evening planned for him." Karma glanced at the wall clock above the door, realized it was two o'clock, and yelped. "I have to go. I still need to stop at the mall to pick up his gift."

"Girl, I understand. No worries. Have fun with Judge Hottie!"

Karma returned to her desk, grabbed her handbag off the floor and tossed her cell phone and wallet inside. Morrison needed to unwind, a distraction to take his mind off his troubles, and Karma had planned a romantic night for him. Yesterday, Morrison and Roderick had had another meeting with investigators at the SEC—their third meeting in three weeks—but nothing had been resolved. Morrison feared the investigation would drag on for months, and Roderick's drinking would get worse. He thought the stress of the insider trading case was weighing heavily on his youngest brother, but Karma disagreed. Roderick missed Toya dearly, and was struggling without her. Sure, he put on a brave face in front of his family and friends, but it was obvious he was lost without the woman he loved. Every day, he seemed more hopeless, and at the banquet he'd talked about his ex-fiancée nonstop.

"I saw the pictures you posted online at the banquet," Jazz said with a toothy smile. "Things must be going really well with you and Morrison if you've already met his family."

Karma turned off the lights and exited her office with Jazz in tow. "Things are great. To be honest, after my dad showed up, I was worried his parents would pressure him to dump me, or threaten to disown him if we continued dating, but they've been incredibly supportive."

"As they should be. You're a strong, intelligent woman with a thriving business, and your dad's paid his debt to society. If someone has a problem with that, screw them!"

"I lost some clients who I guess were uncomfortable with Feisal being an ex-con and didn't like seeing him at the salon, but it's their loss not mine..." Hearing R & B music playing loudly in the salon—her favorite Bruno Mars song—her thoughts drifted away and she trailed off speaking.

Entering the main floor, Karma was struck by the lavish flower bouquets and scented candles all around the salon. Red rose petals were sprinkled on the floor, creating a romantic ambience and fragrant aroma in the air. Everyone was there—her staff, her father, her grandparents, the Drake family—and their excitement was palpable. Reagan waved, Mrs. Drake beamed and Abigail mouthed the words, "Relax, relate, release." Before Karma could ask her friends and family what was going on, Morrison appeared at her side and took her hand in his. He looked dashing in his black tuxedo and crisp white shirt, like a groom on his wedding day, and the earnest expression on his face made her heart swoon.

"Morrison, what's going on?" she whispered, wishing her palms weren't slick with sweat. "What are you doing here? You're supposed to be in court."

Flashing a sly, bad-boy grin that made his eyes twinkle, he slowly shook his head. "No, beautiful, I'm supposed to be right here with you..."

Her pulse thumped inside her ears, and her thoughts spun out of control. Karma couldn't understand what was happening, and struggled to focus on what Morrison was saying.

Cameras flashed, temporarily blinding her.

"All week, my friends and family have been asking

me what I want for my birthday, and when I gave it some thought I realized the only gift I wanted was you. You mean the world to me, Karma, and I want to spend the rest of my life with you in wedded bliss," he confessed.

Incredibly, tears filled her eyes, blurring her vision, but she didn't cry. "But what about my past? I'm worried if the truth gets out it could embarrass you or ruin your chances to become a Supreme Court judge in the future."

Morrison cupped her chin. "If I could only choose one, I'd choose you."

Their friends and family oohed and ahhed.

After dropping to one knee, he reached into his pocket and took out a small, white box.

"I don't know what the future holds, but as long as we're together, I know it'll be great. You're my heart, Karma, everything I didn't know I wanted in a woman, and I love you more than anything in this world."

Karma choked down a sob, willed herself to keep it together. "I love you too, Morrison. More than I've ever loved anyone, and I feel fortunate to have you in my life."

"Will you give me the best birthday gift I've ever received and agree to marry me?"

"Yes! I'll marry you! I'd love to!" Karma shouted, showering his face with kisses.

Taking her left hand in his, he slid the pink, heart-shaped diamond ring onto her finger, then kissed her palm. Moved by his words, Karma draped her arms around his neck and vowed never to take him for granted. "I love you, baby, and I always will."

"I love you more, Mrs. Morrison Drake-To-Be, and I will cherish and adore you always."

Overcome with joy and happiness, Karma wiped the tears from her eyes and gazed up at her new fiancé. *How did I ever get so lucky?* she wondered, caressing his handsome face. *Morrison not only reunited me and my father, he taught me how to forgive and love unconditionally, and for that I'm deeply grateful.*

"I want you to be my wife, and have my babies." Morrison winked. "Two of each sex would be nice."

Karma whispered in his ear, "It's never too early to practice, so when we get to your estate, it's on!"

Surrounded by friends and family, they shared a sweet, tender kiss on the lips, and as Morrison—her real-life Prince Charming—held her close to his chest, Karma realized dreams really *did* come true.

* * * * *

KIMANI™
ROMANCE

COMING NEXT MONTH
Available June 19, 2018

#577 UNDENIABLE ATTRACTION
Burkes of Sheridan Falls • by Kayla Perrin
When a family wedding reunites Melissa Conwell with Aaron Burke, she's determined to prove she's over the gorgeous soccer star who broke her heart years before. Newly single Aaron wants another chance with Melissa and engineers a full-throttle seduction. Will Melissa risk heartbreak again for an elusive happily-ever-after?

#578 FRENCH QUARTER KISSES
Love in the Big Easy • by Zuri Day
Pierre LeBlanc is a triple threat: celebrated chef, food-network star and owner of the Big Easy's hottest restaurant. Journalist Rosalyn Arnaud sees only a spoiled playboy not worthy of front-page news. Their attraction tells another story. But when she uncovers his secret, their love affair could end in shattering betrayal…

#579 GUARDING HIS HEART
Scoring for Love • by Synithia Williams
Basketball star Kevin Koucky plans to end his career by posing naked in a magazine feature. When photographer Jasmine Hook agrees to take the assignment, she never expects a sensual slam dunk. But he comes with emotional baggage. Little does she know that Kevin always plays to win…

#580 A TASTE OF PLEASURE
Deliciously Dechamps • by Chloe Blake
Italy is the perfect place for new beginnings—that's what chef Danica Nilsson hopes. But one look at Antonio Dante Lorenzetti and her plan to keep romance out of her kitchen goes up in flames. The millionaire restaurateur wants stability. Not unbridled passion. Is she who he's been waiting for?

Get 2 Free Books,
Plus 2 Free Gifts—
just for trying the
Reader Service!

"This is certainly going to be one interesting weekend," she muttered.

"It sure is."

A jolt hit Melissa's body with the force of a soccer ball slamming into her chest. That voice… A tingling sensation spread across her shoulder blades. It was a voice she hadn't heard in a long time. Deeper than she remembered, but it most definitely belonged to *him*.

Holding her breath, she turned. And there he was. Aaron Burke. Looking down at her with a smile on his face and a teasing glint in his eyes.

"I thought that was you," he said, his smile deepening.

Melissa stood there looking up at him from wide eyes, unsure what to say. Why was he grinning at her as though he was happy to see her?

"It's good to see you, Melissa."

Aaron spread his arms wide, an invitation. But Melissa stood still, as if paralyzed. With a little chuckle, Aaron stepped forward and wrapped his arms around her.

Melissa's heart pounded wildly. Why was he doing this? Hugging her as if they were old friends? As if he hadn't taken her virginity and then broken her heart.

"So we're paired off for the wedding," Aaron said as he broke the hug.

"So we are," Melissa said tersely. She was surprised that she'd found her voice. Her entire body was taut, her head light. She was mad at herself for having any reaction to this man.

"You're right. It's going to be a very interesting weekend indeed," Aaron said, echoing her earlier comment.

He looked good. More than good. He looked…delectable. Six feet two inches of pure Adonis, his body honed to perfection. Wide shoulders, brawny arms fully visible in his short-sleeved dress shirt and a muscular chest. His strong upper body tapered to a narrow waist. A wave of heat flowed through Melissa's veins, and she swallowed at the uncomfortable sensation. She quickly averted her eyes from his body and took a sip of champagne, trying to ignore the warmth pulsing inside.

Good grief, what was wrong with her? She should be immune to Aaron's good looks. And yet she couldn't deny the visceral response that had shot through her body at seeing him again.

It was simply the reaction of a female toward a man who was amazingly gorgeous. She wasn't dead, after all. She could find him physically attractive even if she despised him.

Although *despised* was too strong a word. He didn't matter to her enough for her to despise him.

Still, she couldn't help giving him another surreptitious once-over. He had filled out—everywhere. His arms were bigger, his shoulders wider, his legs more muscular. His lips were full and surrounded by a thin goatee—and good Lord, did they ever look kissable…

Don't miss UNDENIABLE ATTRACTION
by Kayla Perrin, available July 2018
wherever Harlequin® Kimani Romance™
books and ebooks are sold.

Want to give in to temptation with steamy tales of irresistible desire?

Check out **Harlequin® Presents®**, **Harlequin® Desire** and **Harlequin® Kimani™ Romance** books!

New books available every month!